Bug Out!
Texas Book 2
The New Republic

Robert Boren

South Bay Press

Book Layout ©2017 BookDesignTemplates.com
Bug Out! Texas Part 2 – The New Republic/ Robert Boren. -- 1st ed.
ISBN 9781520296005

To Roger

Contents

Previously – in Bug Out! Texas Book 1

Something was wrong in Texas. A terror attack hit the Superstore in Dripping Springs. The attack was foiled by a group of armed citizens, rednecks led by Kelly, and off-duty Austin cops Jason Finley and Kyle Wilson. After the battle, Islamists behind the attack located those who'd foiled it, killing several, but being killed in large numbers by Jason and his wife Carrie, as well as Kelly and his band of rednecks. This enraged the Islamist leaders. They staged a major attack at a protest in Austin the next day. Kelly and his friends showed up and helped the Austin PD kill them. Meanwhile, Jason and his family and Kyle and his girlfriend Kate were ordered into hiding by their boss, Chief Ramsey. They took off in RVs with the enemy hot on their trail.

The Islamists tracked down Jason's parents at their ranch outside Fredericksburg and beheaded them. Jason told his brother Eric about the murders. Eric and his girlfriend Kim traveled from Florida in their motor home to help, but were stopped at the Texas border outside of Houston. They traveled north along the Texas/Louisiana border until they found a place to cross into Texas, while being hunted by Islamic fighters. Eric noticed the enemy, set up an ambush, and killed them. After the battle he discovered that they had been tracked by a virus on their cellphones. He warned Jason, who in turn warned Austin PD and Kelly. In the last scene of book one, Jason and Kyle used their hacked cellphones to lure the Islamists into an ambush.

Meanwhile, Venezuelan troops and Islamist fighters were flooding across the border into Texas via Falcon Lake. Department of Public Safety Patrol Boaters did battle with the invaders. They stopped many but lost boats and men in firefights, as the invaders got more powerful. Texas National Guard leadership joined with DPS to fight off the invaders, using Juan Carlos Gonzales and Brendon Smith as pilots for new equipment and tactics. They did serious damage to the enemy, but their boat got disabled on the Mexican side of Falcon Lake at the end of book one.

Kip Hendrix, President Pro Tempore of the Texas State Senate, was alarmed at the battles with Islamist/Venezuelan forces and the resulting pressure on the Muslim community in Austin. He conspired with other like-minded political figures to shut down those he considered to be vigilantes, and to attack the loose gun laws of Texas which were helping them. When Hendrix realized that the invasion was, in fact, a true invasion of foreign fighters from Venezuela and the Islamic countries of the Middle East, he publicly joined the Texas Patriots and vowed to fight the enemy with them. Behind closed doors, he had other ideas.

{ 1 }

Barracuda

Carrie and Kate were dozing in the motor home. It was late, nearly two in the morning. Dingo was sleeping on the engine cover between the front seats. Her head lifted, looking around, making a low growl.

Kate woke up and looked at Dingo, heart beating faster. "Carrie!" she whispered loud.

Carrie woke and looked at Kate. "What? Hear something?"

"Dingo just growled," she whispered.

"Probably a hog," Carrie said, eyes drowsy. She drifted off again when the pop of gunfire sounded in the distance.

"Crap," Kate said, sitting up.

"The guys!" Carrie said, standing.

More gunfire drifted towards them. Automatic fire from big weapons.

"BARs," Carrie said. "It's happening. Let's get our guns ready just in case."

"Wow, that's a lot of gunfire," Kate said, rushing towards the dinette table. She picked up one of the Thompsons and a box of ammo. Carrie grabbed her Mini-14 with one hand and a shotgun with the other.

"I'm going on the roof of the motor home," Carrie said. She left a sleeping Chelsea in the bedroom, and then left the coach, heading for the ladder on the back.

"Be careful up there," Kate said. "I'll get behind the bushes in front of the trailer with one of the Thompsons."

"Maybe I better bring the other Thompson up here," Carrie said. She climbed up the ladder and slid the Mini-14 and the shotgun onto the roof, then ran back into the coach and grabbed her Thompson. She was on the roof in a flash.

"You set?" Kate asked.

"Yeah," Carrie said, pulling back the bolt on the Thompson and setting it aside. She picked up the Mini-14 and laid on her belly, watching down the road.

The gunfire went on for several minutes, then stopped for a moment, a few short bursts of fire sounding every so often. Both women stayed still, listening.

"Think it's over?" Kate asked.

"Listen. Vehicles. You hear it?"

More gunfire from the BARs floated towards them, and the engines of the vehicles accelerated.

"Somebody's coming," Kate said. "Oh, God."

Trucks came into view, flying towards them in the darkness. Carrie took aim with the Mini-14, squeezing the trigger, trying to hit the driver of the first truck.

"The trucks are bouncing too much," Carrie said. "I can't hit them." She continued to fire, and then Kate stood up behind the bushes and fired the Thompson, sweeping fire across the front of the first truck, killing all three men in the cab. Men leapt out of the truck bed in a panic.

"Use the machine gun," Kate yelled as she continued to fire, trying to stop the second truck now.

Carrie grabbed the Thompson and fired, hitting men around the first truck as it rolled onto the side of the road.

"That second truck is still coming," Kate said. She fired again, hitting the driver. The truck stopped, and somebody inside opened the car door and shoved the dead driver out, getting behind the wheel, driving forward in a panicked zig-zag, making it hard for Kate to hit them. Her firing stopped.

"What's wrong?" Carrie yelled.

"Damn thing jammed," she shouted.

Carrie's heart was hammering in her chest. She opened fire on the second truck until it was too close, then shot at the third truck, hitting the engine compartment. Steam blew out of the radiator but it kept coming, zig-zagging like the second truck.

"They're going to get us," Kate cried, trying frantically to put the magazine back on the Thompson. Suddenly there was an explosion, hitting the second truck, blowing it into the air.

"What was that?" Carrie cried. She turned and saw a small off-roader flying down the road from the back side of camp, a cannon mounted above the roll cage. A bright flash erupted from the big gun and the third truck blew up in a huge fireball.

"Who is that?" Kate yelled as she rammed the magazine back into the Thompson. She pulled back the bolt and opened fire, hitting the men who were fleeing from the burning wreck.

"Nice shooting," Carrie shouted. There were three men sprinting towards the motor home, trying to take aim at her. She picked up Jason's auto shotgun and fired as fast as she could, killing them as Kate continued to fire the Thompson. There was silence for a moment, and then a Jeep was driving towards them full bore.

"Another one?" Kate yelled.

"No, it's our Jeep. Hold you fire!"

Carrie watched as the Jeep skidded to a stop and Kyle leapt out, firing his BAR at two men trying to get away to the right. Jason jumped out too, looking around with the night-vision goggles, checking the bushes.

"They okay?" Kate asked.

"Yeah, they just wasted a few stragglers," Carrie said. "Where's that dune buggy?"

"Right here," shouted a man's voice.

"Curt!" Carrie said. "Thank God."

"That Jason and Kyle mopping up?"

"Yeah," Carrie said.

Jason and Kyle rushed over. Kate got up, running to Kyle, leaping into his arms as he dropped his weapon, arms around his neck, legs around his waist. She cried and kissed him and touched his face.

Carrie came down the steps of the ladder and rushed into Jason's arms, hugging him and sobbing. They could hear Chelsea crying inside the coach. "I'd better go to her." She ran into the coach.

"Jason!" Curt said, walking towards him.

"Man, am I glad to see you," he said. The men embraced.

"I got here none too soon, but your women were putting up one hell of a fight."

"What is that thing?" Jason asked, looking at the dune buggy behind him.

"Oh, just a little toy I cooked up," he said.

Kyle came over with Kate. "Curt, we owe you big time," Kyle said.

"Hell, I owe you," he said. "A truckload of these cretins was almost to me when I figured out their phone hack. If you wouldn't have tipped me off, I'd be dead right now."

"You figured it out?" Kate asked.

"Oh, this is my girlfriend," Kyle said. "Kate."

"I'm your girlfriend now?" Kate asked.

"You have a problem with that?" Kyle asked.

She looked at him, eyes teary, and shook her head no.

Curt laughed. "Somebody finally nailed him, huh?"

"Looks like it to me," Jason said. "It's a good thing."

"Yes it is," Kyle said, pulling Kate close.

"Well, great to meet you, Kate."

Kyle smiled. "Now what were you saying about the phones?"

"I figured out how to see who was tracking me. Saw them coming."

"I figured you'd be able to do that," Kyle said. "I have one of the Islamist's phones on me. Android. Took out the battery. Maybe you can use it."

"Yeah, maybe I can," Curt said. "There's probably other numbers stored in it that I can hack into."

"Can you tell if there's people on the way here now?" Kate asked.

"Yeah," he said. "Rigged up my phone so it'll buzz if any phones I haven't input get within half a mile. Wouldn't work in the city, but out here it's perfect."

Carrie came back out.

"She okay?" Jason asked.

"Yeah, she's back asleep already. What'd I miss?"

"Curt figured out how to use the hacked phones against the Islamists," Jason said.

"Really?" Carrie asked.

"Yeah," Curt said. "It's pretty simple."

"Is he a genius?" Kate asked.

Curt laughed. "No, but I read a lot. Come check out my new toy."

"Yeah, what the hell is that thing?" Carrie asked.

"Just your basic Barracuda dune buggy, but I added some extra hardware. C'mon."

They walked over to the vehicle. Curt pulled out his cellphone and turned on the flashlight, shining it on the strange looking buggy. "I built the vehicle from a kit. Single seater, faster than hell in the dirt, small profile in the front so it's hard to hit with gunfire."

"Nice," Kyle said. "Wouldn't want to roll it though. That would be the end of the gun up on the roll cage."

"I've got an idea for a better roll cage," Curt said, "but it's low priority. If I'm in action and I roll it, I'm probably dead anyway. There's other improvements I have in mind that are more important."

"Where did you get that gun, and that gimbal mount?" Jason asked.

"The gun is a Mark 19, mod 3 automatic 40 mm grenade launcher," Curt said. "Rather not say where I got it. I've got more. We're gonna need them. The ammo is the hardest problem, but I got some ideas on that."

"I've read about these," Jason said. "How about the gimbal?"

Curt laughed and got into the buggy. He pulled down a sight, which went in front of his face. "Buttons on either side of the steering wheel control the gimbal. Up-down on one, left-right on the other. Takes some practice. It's connected to the cross hairs on this sight. The left-right button is also the trigger." He pushed the ignition button. The engine started, settling into a purr. Then Curt used the buttons to move the gun around.

"Holy shit," Kyle said.

"I made the gimbal and sight parts with my 3-D Printer, which is in the back of my toy hauler," Curt said.

"What was your idea on the ammo?" Kyle asked.

"I'm trying to reverse engineer it. I think I can make a lot of the parts with my 3-D printing setup. Not the best way to manufacture, but it's workable. I save the shell casings when I can."

"Hate to stop the reunion here, but we need to figure out what we're going to do tonight," Carrie said. "We're low on sleep, and the enemy knows where we are."

"She's right," Jason said. "We need to split, right?"

"That would be advisable," Curt said.

"Where's your rig?" Kyle asked.

"Three hundred yards down the road," Curt said. "I can be ready to go in a hurry. All I have to do is drive the Barracuda into the back."

"Not much we have to do either," Jason said. "Throw the patio stuff into the storage compartments. Hitch the vehicles back up. Ten minutes."

"Where should we go?" Kyle asked.

"West," Curt said. "Talked with some old friends. That's where they're going."

"Old friends?" Kate asked.

"Don't tell me, let me guess," Jason said. "Kelly and his band of rednecks."

Curt grinned.

"You sure that's a good idea?" Carrie asked. "Doesn't that put all the targets together in the same place?"

"Yeah," Curt said. "It'll drag them right into the lion's den."

Shoreline

It was early morning on Falcon Lake. Juan Carlos and Brendan were stranded on the shore.

"What do you think?" Brendan asked, wading into the water. Juan Carlos was looking at the engines.

"We were lucky, dude," Juan Carlos said. "Looks like they shot the stern armor, and the bullet bounced off and nicked the fuel feeder line."

"Can you fix it?"

"Temporarily," he said. "I need the tape. It's in the tool box. Want to grab it for me?"

"Sure," Brendan said. He got into the boat and looked under the row of seats in the back, pulling out a small toolbox. "Found it. Here."

Juan Carlos reached up and got the roll of tape. "Any safety wire left? The adhesive might come loose."

"Yeah," Brendan said. He fished a spool of the wire and the pliers out of the box and put them on the stern.

"Wonder what happened at the base?" Juan Carlos asked.

"Don't know, man, but it was bad. You had the radio on?"

"No, I turned it off last night to save the battery," he said. "If we get the engines running again, we'd better make a call right away."

"Seriously," Brendan said, watching the shore and the water. "How long till they find us?"

"You worry too much, dude," Juan Carlos said. "I'm just about done." He finished with the tape and then wrapped it with the safety wire, being careful not to twist too tight. "That ought to do it."

Brendan watched as Juan Carlos waded out of the water and climbed on the bow.

"You'll have to push us off," Juan Carlos said. He slipped into the pilot seat and pushed the ignition button. The engines turned, grinding a few moments and catching, settling into their raspy purr.

"Bitchen," Brendan said. "I'll push us off." He scrambled off the bow and jumped onto the sand, heaving with all his might as Juan Carlos put the engines into reverse and gave them gas. Brendan jumped back on when they were floating free.

"Hey, dude, go look at the tubing. Make sure it's not leaking, okay?"

"Yeah," Brendan said, rushing to the stern. He peered over. "Looks good, man. Let's blow this joint."

"USA here we come," Juan Carlos said, pushing the throttle forward. "See if you can get somebody on the radio."

Brendan nodded as they cut into the center of the lake, flipped on the radio power button, and picked up the mic. "Zapata, come in. Over."

Nothing but static hiss.

"Keep trying," Juan Carlos said.

"Zapata, come in. Over."

"Switch channels, dude."

"Yeah," Brendan said. He turned the dial. "DPS, come in. Over."

"This is DPS. Who's on? Over."

"Gonzales and Smith, boat 18. Over."

"Where's Chauncey? Over."

"Dead. Shot by a sniper off Arroyo Chapote. What happened to Zapata Base? Over."

"Attacked last night. The enemy took control of the lake north of Rio Salado. Over."

"So we're just gonna let them do that? Over."

"Negative, we have forces taking the base back now, and air support on the way. Over."

Brendan looked over at the Zapata base, still smoking. There was a firefight going on, with a barge and a cutter off shore pouring fire at the vehicles driving onto the base.

"I see the battle going on. We're a mile away. Still have SMAW rockets. Need help? Over."

"Where did you get rockets? Over."

"Chauncey. Over."

"Yes, attack if you can, but get away afterwards. Very few boats left. Over and out."

"Getting us into trouble again," Juan Carlos said. "Load the SMAW and get up front. We're going in hot."

"Roger that," Brendan said, picking up the launcher and pushing a rocket into place. "I'm loaded."

Juan Carlos pointed the boat towards the cutter first, flooring the engine.

"This is great, dude," Brendan said. "They are concentrating on the shoreline, and they can't hear us above the gunfire."

"Get ready," Juan Carlos shouted. "I'll cut the engine right when we get there."

"Don't bother, man. I can hold it fine like this, as long as we don't hit any chop."

"Good," Juan Carlos said as they raced towards the boats.

"Got you," Brendan said, pulling the trigger. The rocket flew towards the back of the cutter, hitting the stern and blowing the back half of the boat off. Brendan reloaded.

"Hit that barge, then we'll finish both of them off, dude."

"Way ahead of you," Brendan said, firing the rocket, reloading before it struck the target.

"Direct hit!" Juan Carlos shouted as the barge exploded.

"Keep us going towards that cutter," Brendan said. "Needs another shot."

"On it," Juan Carlos said. He made a sweeping turn back towards it, and Brendan fired, the rocket hitting the boat broadside, exploding the midsection. It sank right away, men screaming and diving off.

"One more for the barge," Brendan said, loading and firing another rocket. It hit the smoking hulk of the barge and exploded, touching off the gasoline tanks, making a huge fireball.

"Yes!" Juan Carlos shouted, shaking his fist. "Burn baby burn!"

"I'm getting on the gun," Brendan said, getting to his feet and aiming the starboard side gun. He opened fire, hitting as many men in the water as he could, then firing on the enemy fighters rushing to the dock. The DPS and Texas National Guard vehicles flooded into place and opened fire, clearing the dock and rushing into the ruins of the headquarters building.

"We're done," Juan Carlos said. "I'm getting back on the radio. Stay on the gun, and keep an eye out on the Mexican side, just in case."

"Yeah," Brendan said. He fired more rounds at the men in the water who were swimming towards the dock.

"DPS, come in. Over."

"Boat 18? Over."

"Yeah, it's Gonzales. Over."

"How'd you do? Over."

"Barge and cutter sank. DPS and Texas National Guard ground forces taking the base. Over."

"Stay sharp. There are four more cutters and *who knows how many* barges on the water. Over."

"Where should we go? To the dock at Zapata? Over."

"Negative. Can you make it to OPEC Creek? Over."

"Probably, as long as the patch I put on the fuel line holds. Over."

"Give it a try. We need to preserve the boats. We've set up a field headquarters at OPEC. They can repair the fuel line and resupply you. Over."

"Okay, we're on our way. Over."

"Where is Chauncey's body? Over."

"On the deck. Over."

"Okay, Gonzales, see you soon. Over and out."

"What the hell is going on?" Brendan said. "Where's the damn air support?"

"I smell the Feds, dude," Juan Carlos said. They headed to OPEC full bore.

{ 3 }

Westward

Kelly sipped coffee, one hand on the wheel of his truck. Brenda was nestled next to him in the middle, Junior sitting against the passenger side door.

"Which way we going again?" Junior asked.

"Through Fredericksburg," Kelly said.

"Isn't that where the cop's parents got killed?" Brenda asked. "Maybe we should go a different way."

"She's got a point, Kelly," Junior said.

"My phone wasn't hacked," she said. "Should I look at the GPS?"

"Yeah, honey, go for it," Kelly said. Junior snickered.

"What's so funny?" Brenda asked.

"*Honey.* You two are turning into an old married couple before my eyes."

"Oh, please," Brenda said as she looked at her phone. "Almost dawn."

"Yeah, we'll have light pretty quick. I'm gonna have to pull over in the next town and check the wheel bearings on the trailer. Feels a little gritty."

"They shot?" Junior asked.

"I don't think so, but they might be a little dry. This trailer hasn't moved for about six years."

"Tires might be suspect too," Junior said.

"Could be," Kelly said. "What's the next town, *honey?*"

Brenda giggled. "You know, I actually kinda like that."

"Told you," Junior said. "When you getting hitched?"

"Been there, done that," Brenda said.

"One step at a time," Kelly said, resting his hand on Brenda's leg. She glanced over at him, soft smile on her face.

"You'd consider it?" she asked.

He smiled back at her but didn't say a word. Junior snickered again.

"Shut up, Junior," Brenda said. "It's gonna be hard to avoid Fredericksburg if we want to go west on Interstate 10. We'd have to go way south on Highway 281."

"What's *way south?*" Junior asked.

"All the way down to State Road 473," she said. "Ever been on that road? We'd be on it a long time going west."

Junior laughed. "Oh, yeah, the old *Farm to Market* road. If I was with the Islamists, I'd love to catch somebody there. Dozens of great places for an ambush."

"What's the alternative?" Kelly asked.

"Stay on Highway 290 as it turns north through Johnson City," she said. "We're getting close to there now. Then west through Fredericksburg, and on to I-10."

"Hmmm," Kelly said. "I'd rather run into these creeps on 290 or I-10 than on the *Farm to Market* road."

Brenda sighed. "I agree. We're only about twenty minutes from Johnson City. Think you can wait that long on the bearings?"

"Yeah," Kelly said. "I've been driving under fifty-five most of the way. Maybe I'll get new tires there too, just in case. They got anybody selling stuff like that?"

"I'll take a look," Brenda said.

"Wonder where the rest of the guys are?" Junior asked.

"Good question," Kelly said. "Wish we all had cellphones."

"We should buy new ones when we're in town," Brenda said.

"Yeah, I was thinking either that or a GPS unit for the truck," Kelly said.

"GPS unit might be better," Junior said. "Don't think they can hack that, and they're hands-free."

"Here's a place – big RV dealership with gas station and repair bays. Just off Main Street a few blocks."

"Main Street?" Kelly asked.

"Main Street is Highway 290," Brenda said. "They got a diner next door. We can get a bite while we're there."

"Yeah, I could use some pancakes," Junior said.

"And more coffee," Kelly said. "The thermos is about empty."

They drove along for another few miles, seeing more and more buildings as the town got closer. Soon they were in the town, traffic slowing as people rushed to work.

"What time is it?" Kelly asked. Brenda looked at her phone.

"Almost eight," she said. "See that street with the light coming up? Turn right."

"Okay," Kelly said, slowing down. He made the turn and saw the big RV dealership on his left. "Don't think they're open yet."

"The diner is," Junior said. "See it? Just past the lot."

Kelly drove onto the RV lot and pulled next to the door. "Says they open at nine. Gives us an hour for breakfast. I'm gonna park over there, see?" He pointed to some long angled RV parking places.

"Perfect," Brenda said.

"Look at those used motor homes over there," Junior said. "I'm gonna check them out when they open."

"You in the market?" Kelly asked.

"Seems like a good time," Junior said.

Kelly parked and they walked to the diner. It was busy, but they got a table. Brenda rushed to the women's room.

"You really got her hornswoggled," Junior said, sliding into the booth across from Kelly. He laughed.

"I think it's the other way around," Kelly said. "Nice feeling."

"She's got a temper."

"I know," Kelly said, picking up a menu. "Don't care."

"You don't care *now*," he said. "I must admit that I'm a little jealous, though."

"You'll get over it," Kelly said. "Here she comes."

"What were you two talking about?" Brenda asked as she slid in next to Kelly.

"Nothing," Kelly said. "Just boy talk, you know."

Junior snickered, and Brenda rolled her eyes.

"I hope this wasn't a mistake."

"It won't be," Kelly said, slipping his arm around her shoulders. She leaned against him.

The waitress walked over and took their order, then scurried away. They chatted and enjoyed breakfast, waiting for the RV dealership to open.

"Getting tired, sweetie?" Kelly asked.

"A little," she said. "Maybe we ought to find a place to camp before it gets too late. Catch up on sleep."

"It's *sweetie* now?" Junior asked.

"Junior, am I gonna have to listen to this forever?" Brenda asked.

"Oh, I'm just teasing," Junior said. "I'm happy for you two. Really."

"Look, the dealership's opening," Kelly said, pointing out the window.

"Good," Brenda said. "Why don't you two go ahead, and I'll settle up."

"Need some dough?" Kelly asked.

"Nah, we're good. Grabbed plenty of cash on the way out of the bar last night. The place *is* half mine, you know."

"Okay, thanks," Kelly said. Brenda slid out of the booth and let Kelly out. He and Junior walked out the door, crossing onto the RV dealership parking lot. Brenda watched them for a moment, her eyes on Kelly's confident stride.

"He's mine," she whispered to herself.

"You all done?" the waitress asked.

"Yes," she said. The waitress handed her the check.

"Thanks." Brenda left a tip on the table and walked to the register. An older woman was running the register.

"Everything okay?" she asked.

"Very good," Brenda said. "Is there a cellphone store in town?"

"Yeah, all the major carries have stores, a little further down on Main Street. Probably don't open until ten, though."

"Thanks," Brenda said. She left, meeting Kelly as he headed to the rig.

"Hey, Brenda," Kelly said.

"They gonna take care of you?" she asked.

"Yeah, they suggested new tires because of their age, and they'll check the bearings. I think it's good idea. They'll fill the propane tanks for us too."

"Good," Brenda said. "Where's Junior?"

"He's talking to a salesman about that motor home over there." He pointed to an old Winnebago Brave.

"I remember those," Brenda said. "Looks kinda old. We ain't gonna be helping him with a breakdown every few miles, I hope."

"Junior is pretty careful when there's money involved," Kelly said.

"He's got money?" Brenda asked. "He should spend it on clothes."

Kelly chuckled. "He's set pretty well. Out-lived his brother and sister, and neither of them had heirs. He got a big chunk of cash from the sale of his dad's ranch."

They got into the truck, and Kelly drove to the service building, backing the trailer into a bay as the mechanic guided him.

"I talked to the cashier about cell phones. She said there's places further down Main Street."

"Good," Kelly said. "You want to sleep a little? I'm gonna watch the mechanic. You can lay down in here."

"I'll try," Brenda said. "Don't you get too tired. We really should find somewhere close by to rest."

"I'll ask the folks here if there's good places, okay?"

"Okay," she said. He left the cab, and she laid down. The mechanic already had the first wheel off.

"Good thing you stopped when you did," he said. "This bearing was way too dry. Would've lost it if you kept going."

"I was afraid of that. Will they be okay with new grease, or should I change them out?"

"If it were me, I'd change them out just to be sure. It's not very expensive, and it's quick."

"Let's do it then," Kelly said. "I want this to be reliable."

"Nice trailer," he said. "How's the inside?"

"Getting a little tired, but it's usable," Kelly said. "I replaced the fridge fairly recently. The air conditioner could be better."

"We sell those," the mechanic said. "They're not cheap, though."

"How much?" Kelly asked.

"Just a sec," he said. "Got to take a look. Hey Rudy, get over here and change these wheel bearings, okay? Oh, and pull that power line over and plug it into the trailer."

A young Hispanic man nodded and rushed over. Kelly and the mechanic went inside the trailer to look at the air conditioner.

"Turn it on."

Kelly switched the electrical on and then adjusted the thermostat to start the air conditioner. The unit came on, and they stood under it as it warmed up.

"Sounds okay," the mechanic said. "Good and cold. It doesn't keep up with the demand?"

"Not so well, at least in the summer," Kelly said.

"It's probably the insulation. These old trailers aren't the best for that."

"Oh," Kelly said. "Anything I can do about it?"

"Yeah, but it's a big deal. Got to take the interior walls off and put in more insulation material. You'd be better off getting a better trailer."

"Okay," Kelly said. "We'll see, then. Thanks."

The men came out, and the mechanic started the second wheel while Rudy finished off the first one.

Junior walked into the bay, twirling keys, grinning ear to ear.

"You did it, didn't you?" Kelly asked.

"Yep, I'm now the proud owner of an RV," he said. "Got a good deal, too."

"You won't be breaking down on us every five minutes, right? That rig is old."

"Rebuilt motor and tranny," Junior said. "I wouldn't have bought it if not for that."

"Run good?" Kelly asked.

"Purrs like a kitten," he said. "How's it going with the trailer?"

"New tires and bearings," Kelly said. "Figured it was worth it. We're gonna be in these rigs for a while."

"Yeah, I'm looking at that coach out there as my new home," he said. "Wish I would've had her before we left. I could have loaded her up with just about everything I own."

"We'll get back there eventually," Kelly said. "Brenda said there's a cellphone shop further down Main Street."

"Good," Junior said. "At least we'll be able to talk to each other again. You still thinking about a GPS unit?"

"Yeah," Kelly said. "Just in case they can find our phones and hack them somehow."

"Well, the Brave has a GPS unit mounted on the dash," Junior said. "Not sure if it works. I'll try it. They're washing her right now. Oh, and they sell GPS units in the store, if you want one."

Brenda got out of the cab.

"Couldn't sleep?" Kelly asked.

"Nah, too keyed up," she said. "I checked on RV Parks. You okay with going just a short distance?"

"How short?" Kelly asked.

"Stonewall," she said. "There's a nice looking RV Park on Cemetery Road."

"Hey, I wouldn't mind that," Junior said. "I'll stock up on some stuff here, and hit a grocery store too. Then I can get my rig set up this afternoon and be ready for a nice long drive tomorrow."

"You bought the rig, didn't you?" Brenda asked.

"Yep," he said. "She's a beauty."

"Good," Brenda said. "We should do some grocery shopping too, Kelly."

"Yeah," Kelly said. "Wonder if they'll let us check in a little early? Check-in is usually three in the afternoon."

"I'll call them," Brenda said. "Want me to make reservations for you too, Junior?"

"Yes, please," he said.

"Okay," Brenda said, walking away with her phone to her ear.

"I'm going into the store," Junior said. "Got a 10% discount after buying the rig."

"Have fun," Kelly said. "I'll come find you when the trailer's done."

Junior nodded and walked away.

"So, your buddy bought the old Brave, huh?" the mechanic said.

"Yep," Kelly said. "Hope he made a good choice."

"He did," the mechanic said. "Rebuilt that motor myself. Tranny came from a good shop. Friend of the owner. Ought to be pretty bullet-proof."

"Hope so," Kelly said. "Or I'll be fixing her. Junior isn't mechanically inclined."

"Trust me, you won't have problems," the mechanic said.

"What's your name, anyway?" Kelly asked. "Mine's Kelly."

"Hank," he said. "Nice to meet you. I'd shake, but you know." He showed his greasy palm.

Kelly chuckled. "Yeah, packed bearings before. I'll leave you to this. How long?"

"Oh, another half hour."

"Good, thanks." Kelly walked towards Brenda. She was just getting off the phone.

"Got us in?" Kelly asked.

"Yeah," she said. "They charge five bucks for early check-in."

"Seriously?" Kelly asked.

"Yep, but it's worth it," she said. "We need the rest."

"Hell, I'd think they would welcome the mid-week business."

"Believe it or not, they're almost full."

"Really?"

"Yeah," Brenda said. "The lady seemed kinda surprised about that herself."

"Shit, people are getting outta Dodge," Kelly said. "We should listen to the radio more. Maybe something else happened in Austin or San Antonio."

"We'll listen when we get back on the road," she said. "We get the cab to ourselves now."

"Yes we do," Kelly said. "Hope I don't bore you."

She smiled at him. "I'm not even a little worried about that."

{ 4 }

Governor's Mansion

Chief Ramsey paced in the reception room, wishing he could fire up a cigar. The mahogany and dark leather furniture in the room reeked of the nineteenth century.

The double pocket doors slid open to either side.

"Chief Ramsey, how are you?" asked Governor Nelson. He walked forward, hand extended. They shook. "Sorry to keep you waiting. Come on in."

The chief followed him into the plush office, sitting in an overstuffed leather chair before the massive desk. The Governor sat behind the desk and leaned back.

"Cigar?" he asked.

Ramsey grinned. "I thought government offices were smoke free, Governor."

"Not this office, dammit," Nelson said, twinkle in his eye. He was a man of average height and build, with salt and pepper hair and chiseled features, clean shaven, eyes set deep.

"Well in that case, hell yes," Ramsey said. The Governor opened a wooden box on his desk, taking out two large cigars, handing one to Ramsey.

"One of life's simple pleasures," Nelson said, biting off the end and spitting it on the floor beside him.

Ramsey laughed and took out his key ring, using his cigar knife to cut the end off of his. The Governor lit up with an ornate 1940s desk lighter and passed it over to the chief.

They both puffed. The chief looked around the office. "Nice digs. You did all right."

"Yeah, look at us now. College screw-ups made good."

The chief laughed. "No way would I have expected this back in the day."

"I knew we'd be here," Nelson said. "You're coming under a lot of pressure from Holly. I even got a call from the US Attorney General's office about you. Couple weeks ago."

"They're still talking to you?" Chief Ramsey asked. "After your stunt with the border?"

"Well, no, as a matter of fact. Not since then. *Not that I care.*"

"How we doing with the bases?"

"We've got them all locked down. Major General Gallagher has full command of all forces located in Texas now, be they state or federal."

"That's got to make you nervous," Ramsey said. "The administration might come in and crush Texas before she's ready."

"The Administration is not legit," Nelson said. *"They know we know.* I think they're more scared of us than we are of them."

"They're not just gonna just let us get away with this," Ramsey said. "They have to do something."

"The US Air Force is no longer under command of the Federal Government."

"What? How?"

"The Administration ordered them to attack US civilians in Southern California," Nelson said. He took a big drag on his cigar. "The leadership of that branch cut off all contact. The entire branch of the service *understands.*"

"Wow," Chief Ramsey said. "How about the other branches?"

"The Administration has also lost control of the Navy. They're sitting things out, watching for foreign intervention. There's been leaks. The US mainland will come under attack. The navy will see to it that the perpetrators are punished."

"Army and Marines?"

"They were the first to be targeted by the invaders, and both are heavily infiltrated. We might have to fight them, but it will only be about one third of those forces, from what General Walker and General Hogan are telling us."

"There's that much resistance to the administration even there, eh?" Ramsey asked. He took a puff. "Hearing bad things about California."

"They're heading for martial law," Nelson said. "Let's just say that the state government there is a little more malleable than most. Lap dogs of the administration."

"What's happening politically to take the traitors down?" Chief Ramsey asked. "There has to be *some* resistance left in the federal government."

"Oh, there is, believe me," Nelson said, "but the situation is gonna get worse before it gets better. The infiltration started there first, and it's been going on for almost ten years. The bureaucracy is filled with traitors. Elected officials are hamstrung. The worst thing to happen was those last three Supreme Court appointments. The Administration is doing a full court press against the Bill of Rights. They're getting no resistance from the judicial branch at all."

"Yeah, those idiots think the people will give up their guns if the Second Amendment gets *re-interpreted*. I think they've got a surprise coming."

"That's an understatement," Nelson said. "Every time they rattle the sabre about that we see gun sales go through the roof. These folks are beyond stupid."

"Yep," Ramsey said. "Why did you want to see me?"

"We're making a temporary move, and I wanted to let you know up front."

"Uh oh, you look serious."

"I'm deadly serious," he said. "I'm declaring Texas to be a Sovereign Republic."

"We're going to secede?" Ramsey said, smile washing over his face.

"You don't look very concerned," the governor said.

"I'm scared shitless, but I think it's a good choice for now. How can I help?"

"Keep an eye on the folks close to the administration. You know who I mean."

"Kip Hendrix and Commissioner Holly," Chief Ramsey said.

"Yeah, they're the two I'm most worried about," he said, "but just so we're clear, I won't tolerate giving anybody a problem because they don't agree with us. Even though we're separating from the federal government for now, the Constitution and Bill of Rights are still firmly in place here. I consider this to be a temporary move, and Texas will help put the

United States together again after this is over. If
somebody takes me out and tries to take advantage of
the situation, I'd like you to do something about it."

"Agreed," he said, "but why do you want me to
keep an eye on Hendrix and Holly if we aren't going
to mess with them?"

"As a sovereign nation, we have to protect
ourselves against enemies from within and without.
Kip and Holly can say whatever they want, can meet
with whoever they want, and can exercise the power
of their positions as they see fit. They can't act as
operatives of the federal government. That's a foreign
government, and acting against Texas using those
connections won't be tolerated."

"So you want me to watch for treason against the
Republic of Texas," Ramsey said.

"Yes," he said. "I'll brief everybody about the
situation, make the case, and ask for
recommendations and objections. Oh, and by the way,
I will stand for reelection in the next cycle. I won't be
a dictator."

"You won't get everybody on your side, even with
your current popularity," Ramsey said. "I won't run a
brown-shirt enforcement operation for you."

"Nor would I ever ask that," Nelson said. "You
know me. We go way back."

"Yes," Ramsey said.

"Good," Nelson said. "I'll hold the first in a series of briefings starting on Thursday morning, and plan to go public on Friday afternoon. I'd like you to be available for the meetings and the public announcement."

"Okay, I'll clear my calendar," Ramsey said. "Who can I tell on the force?"

"Everybody above Sargent right now," he said. "The balance on Thursday morning, before I start the briefings."

"Okay," Ramsey said. "Count me on your side. I'll go meet with my leadership."

"Thanks." Nelson stood up. "Glad you're on board."

The men shook hands, and Ramsey left the office, his head spinning.

East Texas Back Roads

Paco's barking woke Eric.

"What are you barking about?" he asked, sitting up. Paco made a low growl and barked more.

Kim stirred and opened her eyes.

"Something wrong?" she asked.

"Don't think so, but I'd better check." He got out of bed, pulling on his pants and getting into his flip flops on the way to the front of the coach. Paco followed him, still growling. Eric grabbed one of the AKs and looked out the windows.

Kim was up, standing behind him, her Colt Python in her hand. "See anything?" she whispered.

"No," he said. "I'll go check outside."

He cracked the door and peeked out. There was a rustle in the weeds near the front of the coach, and then a grunt. Eric laughed as he saw a young feral pig run away.

"What was it?" Kim asked, looking relieved as she came down the steps in her bare feet.

"Feral pig," Eric said. "If we were gonna be here for a while I'd go get it. The young ones are tasty."

"Oh," she said. "I think Paco needs to go out."

"Yeah," Eric said, reaching in for the leash. "C'mon, fella." He got Paco on the leash and walked outside.

"I'll be with you in a sec," Kim said. Eric nodded as he walked, eyes scanning the area. Nobody in sight.

After a couple minutes Kim joined him. "Beautiful morning."

"Sure is," Eric said. "You look gorgeous."

She smiled. "I'm happy. We gonna take off pretty soon?"

"Yeah, after a little breakfast," Eric said. "Wish we had GPS. Feeling our way around without it is going to be a pain in the ass."

She laughed. "What'd you do out here before GPS?"

"Used paper maps, and got lost quite a bit," he said. "Wish I at least had those maps."

"They aren't stashed somewhere in the coach?"

"Nah, I bought this thing in Florida. Those maps belonged to my dad. They're probably back at the house." Eric's face changed, tears rolling down his cheeks.

"I'm so sorry, honey," Kim said, hugging him. Paco stopped and looked at them, turning his face to the side, trying to understand.

"Don't worry, I'll be okay," Eric said. "I might get like this for a little while, though."

"I understand," Kim said. "Let's find something for breakfast. Saw some eggs when I was in the fridge last night."

"They should still be good," Eric said. "unless they broke during that wild ride we had yesterday."

"Oh yeah," she said. "Why does that seem like so long ago?"

"Don't know," Eric said. "C'mon, Paco, while we're young."

"No rush. I'll get breakfast going," She turned and walked back to the coach as Eric finished off with Paco. He took a quick walk down to the road, looking both directions for signs of anybody. It was deserted. He walked back to the trailer.

"Smells good in here," Eric said. He un-hooked Paco and grabbed his food out of the fridge.

"Saw you walk down to the road. See anybody?"

"No, it's deader than a doornail out there."

"Know where we're going?"

"Yeah, looking at the road in the daylight brought back memories," he said. "That long straight road we were on runs into Oilfield Road. We can take that to a state road with one of those 3000s names. Can't remember the exact number, but I'll know it when I see it." He put to food dish down in front of Paco, who attacked it with vigor.

"I'm glad you're remembering," she said. "Breakfast will be done in a few minutes, and then we can get leave. How long will it take us to get to Deadwood?"

"That's a good question. I don't know. That state road is paved, but the roads leading to it are dirt. Might run into some bad spots. Might run into some people, too. If we run into cops, we'll need a good story for why we're back here."

"You hear that?" Kim asked.

Eric stopped talking and listened. Paco growled.

"Stop, Paco," Eric whispered. "In your bed." Paco held his head low and got into it, turning several times to get comfortable.

"See what it is? Another pig?"

"No, I hear trucks," Eric said. "I'm going out with my binoculars. Stay quiet, okay? Turn off that burner, too. Hopefully the smell doesn't make it down there."

"Good thing there wasn't any bacon," Kim said.

"Seriously." Eric left the cab with the binoculars, creeping along the tree line until he had a good view of the road. He got on his belly and put the binoculars to his eyes, stretching to see around the corner. There was a line of trucks slowly poking along. Troop transport trucks with canvas covers over the backs. They were heading the same direction he planned to drive.

Kim snuck up next to him. "Who is it?"

"I don't know," Eric whispered. "Maybe army. Check it out." He handed the binoculars to her. She looked, moving the focus knob, then gasped.

"What?"

"Islamists. Look. In the back of the last truck."

Eric's heart beat faster. He took the binoculars and focused. There were several men visible in the back of the truck, with white garb and long beards. "Son of a bitch. This is an invasion."

"What do we do?" Kim whispered.

"Well, we can't take them on," he whispered back. "And by the way, they're taking the same road we were going to take."

"You think they're looking for us?"

"No," Eric said. "I think they're sneaking in. Wonder if they'll avoid Deadwood or drive right through it?"

"How big is the town?"

"Small," Eric whispered. "Most of the population lives outside of town, on farms and ranches. Been a while since I've been through there. I'd guess there's less than 200 people."

"And how many men in those trucks?"

"Don't know," Eric whispered. "I counted eight trucks. They probably hold about twelve men each in the back, couple more in the cab."

"Shit, that's over a hundred men," Kim whispered, eyes wide. "What do we do?"

"We wait for a while before we get on the road," Eric said. "That's for sure."

"We don't have phones, so we can't even call anybody."

"Yeah, and this rig is a sitting duck if they see it," Eric said. He thought for a moment. "Maybe we ought to go after them."

"What?" Kim asked. "Are you crazy?"

"We got the Bronco. I could un-hitch it. Leave the motor home here. Tail them. Try to tip off the authorities."

"What if they see us?" Kim asked.

"I'll head into the woods. They won't be able to follow us in those trucks. They'd be on foot. Might even get another good opportunity for an ambush."

"Okay, I'm game. Let's go."

"You should stay here," Eric said.

"Not on your life," Kim said. "If you go, I go. Besides, you need me. I can shoot. Remember?"

Eric was quiet for a moment.

"C'mon," she said. "You didn't really think I'd let you take off without me, did you?"

"No," he said, looking into her face. "You're right. This isn't some little skirmish that will end in a few weeks. This might be our life together for the foreseeable future. I need to show you how the AKs work before we leave, though. We can't go against these guys with lever action hunting rifles and sawed-off shotguns."

"We should take them anyway," Kim said. "What does your brother have?"

Eric laughed. "Well, he's a cop, so he's probably got better arms than we do. Hell, he may have picked up dad's machine guns on the way out of Fredericksburg."

"Your father had machine guns?"

"Yeah, he was a collector. Paid a hefty tax for them. Being an ex-cop helped him get the licenses. But no matter, we're a long way from Jason. We'll be on our own for a while."

"Let's eat and get going," Kim said.

"Yeah," Eric said. "Crap! Get down!"

Kim dropped back under cover and turned towards the road. "More of them?" she whispered.

"This is really bad." Eric watched and counted. "There's another twelve trucks there. How are they getting over the border? That natural gas plant has to be open by now."

"Maybe they killed the workers on the way through."

"God, I hope not," Eric said. "C'mon, let's eat and get on the road."

They went back into the coach and Kim finished cooking the eggs and spam she'd started.

"We taking Paco?" Kim asked.

"Yeah, we have to," Eric said. "We don't know what's gonna happen. We might get tied down somewhere. I don't want him stuck here."

"We should take food for all of us, just in case we don't make it back here."

"Yeah," Eric said. Then he got a grin on his face.

"What?"

"I'm gonna take my archery stuff. I got a nice compound hunting bow and a crossbow."

"Why?" Kim asked.

"We might be able to pick off a straggler," he said. "Get close enough to blow some of their stuff up."

Kim giggled. "We're partisans, aren't we?"

"Damn straight."

{ 6 }

Caravan to West Texas

Jason followed Curt's big toy-hauler on westbound Highway 190, Carrie next to him in the passenger seat. The sun was just coming up.

"Think we can really make it to Fort Stockton today?" Carrie asked. "You got no sleep last night, and I only got an hour."

"I know," Jason said. "Gonna need gas before long."

"I hate not having our cellphones."

"We're coming up on El Dorado," Jason said. "I'll honk my horn and hit my right blinker when we get close to the off-ramp."

"Maybe there's a cellphone store in that town."

"Maybe," Jason said. "There it is." He turned on his right blinker and hit his horn a few times. Curt beeped his horn once and turned his blinker on too.

"Good, he got the message," Carrie said.

"So did Kyle," Jason said.

They took the ramp, heading into the truck stop on the right. Jason parked at a pump and started fueling. Carrie put Dingo on the leash, scooped up Chelsea, and headed for the door.

"Hey, bro," Kyle said, walking up with Kate after Jason started the fuel flowing into his rig.

"Hey," Jason said.

"Where's Carrie?" Kate asked.

"She's walking Dingo. How you guys holding up?"

"I'm tired," Kyle said.

"Me too," Kate said. Curt joined them.

"How you guys doing?" he asked.

"We're getting tired. How much further to Fort Stockton?"

"A few hours," Curt said. "I'm okay with stopping somewhere else on the way, though. We've all been up too long."

Carrie walked up with Dingo and Chelsea. "There's a cellphone store right across the street."

"Really?" Jason asked. "When I'm done fueling I'll pull into one of the parking places in the back."

"Sounds like a plan," Kyle said. "I want a new phone too."

"Yeah," Curt said. "Let's all pull back there. Maybe we could get a bite to eat after we get the phones, and decide where to stop. No reason to push ourselves to Fort Stockton today."

"Good," Carrie said. "I was hoping you'd say that."

"We could probably spend the night here," Jason said. "If there's plenty of spaces back there. Truckers do it all the time."

"That's true," Curt said. "I'd have to use the bathrooms in the truck stop, though."

"Why?" Carrie asked.

"Can't get into my bathroom with the slides closed," he said. "Lot of fifth wheels have that problem. I *can* get to the bed, at least."

"Hell, we could also sleep for a few hours and then make it to Fort Stockton later tonight," Kyle said. "If it's only a few hours away."

"Think about it and we'll talk over breakfast," Jason said.

There was a clunk by Kyle's truck. "Looks like I'm full. I'll see you guys in the back." He took Kate by the hand and went back to their rig.

"Those two really have the hots for each other," Curt said.

"Yep," Jason said. "Never thought I'd see the day."

"She's a looker," Curt said. "Good for him."

"She's good in a fight, too," Carrie said. "Should have seen her with the Thompson last night. Even cleared a jam and went back to fighting."

"Both of you impressed me," Curt said.

The fuel pump clunked in the motor home. "Done," Jason said. "See you back there, Curt."

"Okay," he said. Jason and his family got into the coach, and he drove in back, parking next to Kyle and Kate. There were few big rigs parked there. Curt joined them after a few minutes, and they met outside of their coaches.

"This is pretty good back here," Curt said. "We should talk to the owner, see if we can sleep here for a few hours."

The others nodded, and they walked across the street to the cell phone store. Buying the phones took longer than any of them expected. An hour later they crossed the street and went into the truck stop coffee shop, grabbing a booth towards the front.

"Well, that was an ordeal," Kyle said.

"They had to start from scratch," Jason said. "I hope the enemy can't pick us up again."

"Yeah, it was a pain, but I'm glad we got it done," Carrie said.

The waitress took their orders, then hurried off.

"So what are we doing?" Kate asked. "Want to find a place close by or try to sleep here for a few hours?"

Curt looked at his watch. "Hmmm. It's almost 9:30 now. We'll be in here for around an hour. If we could bed down by 11:00, we could be back on the road by five or six."

"So we'd be at Fort Stockton by seven or eight," Jason said. "Doesn't sound so bad, but can we get to sleep here?"

"There's a good question," Carrie said. "I'll have a hard time getting Chelsea to go down, but I'm not as worried about myself as I am about Jason. He's driving. I could nod off on the way to Fort Stockton."

"There any problem with late check-in at this park in Fort Stockton, Curt?" Jason asked.

"Good question. I'll call them." Curt brought out his new iPhone and searched for the park to get the phone number. "Here it is. Excuse me a minute." He got out of the booth with the phone to his ear.

"More people showing up," Kyle said, looking out the window. "Wonder why? Too early for lunch, too late for morning rush hour."

Curt returned just as the food was arriving. "Well that's a big no-go."

"No late check-in, huh?" Kyle asked.

"No, they're full up," Curt said. "I made us reservations for day after tomorrow. Soonest I could get. I'll try for something close by. Okay?"

"Any port in the storm," Jason said. The others nodded, looking up from their food.

Curt searched as the others ate. "Dammit, no RV Park in El Dorado."

"Really, in this giant metropolis?" Kyle asked.

"Shut up, pencil neck," Curt said. Kate and Carrie grinned at each other.

"Try Sonora," Jason said. "Wouldn't hurt to get on I-10 anyway, so it's not out of the way."

"How far is that?" Carrie asked.

Jason pulled his phone out and checked. "Twenty minutes south, down route 277."

"That's doable," Kate said.

"Sonora it is," Curt said, searching for a park. "Well, there *is* an RV Park." He snickered.

"What?" Carrie asked.

"It's at Highway 271 and West 2nd Street, right across the street from a junk yard."

Jason laughed. "Sounds like a garden spot."

Carrie looked it up. "I see it. Not so bad. It's got a swimming pool across the street too."

"I'll call them," Curt said. He got up and walked away again, phone to his ear.

"Pencil neck?" Kate asked. She giggled.

"Curt has his own unique vocabulary," Carrie said. "Some of it will peel paint, though. That's why I had Jason warn him about Chelsea."

"What, mommy?" Chelsea asked.

"Sometimes Uncle Curt says bad words," Jason said. "Just ignore him if you hear them. Don't repeat it."

"Okay," Chelsea said, eating the last of her grilled cheese sandwich. "This was good. Can I have desert?"

"No, honey, not now," Carrie said. "Maybe after dinner, okay? There are some popsicles in the freezer."

"Okay," she said. "When's dinner?"

Kate laughed.

Curt walked back over and sat. "We're in luck. They have spaces for us, so I made reservations for tonight. The old guy who runs the place is a real hoot."

"Good," Jason said.

The group finished eating, got up to pay the bill, then headed for the door to the back parking lot. Jason stopped on the way out.

"What?" Carrie asked.

"Wow, is that a payphone?"

"Holy shit, there *are* still a few around," Kyle said. "Want to make a call?"

"Yeah, to Chief Ramsey," Jason said. "You guys go ahead. I'll try it. Think I have a few quarters."

"I have some in my purse, too," Carrie said. "I'll wait with you." Chelsea stood by her side, leaning against her, looking sleepy.

Jason picked up the phone receiver while the others went to their rigs.

"It's got a dial tone. I'll call the Austin switchboard." He inserted coins and punched in the number.

"Austin Police Department," the operator said.

"Could I talk to Chief Ramsey, please?"

"I'll see if he's taking calls. Who is this?"

"Officer Finley," Jason said.

"Thank you. Hold the line, please."

There was a click. Jason waited, leaned up against the wall. Then there was another click.

"Officer Finley, so glad to hear from you."

"Hello, sir," he said. "You understood my message?"

"Yes, and thanks," Chief Ramsey said. "Our phones have been replaced, but we never found out who infected them or how, so I'm worried that they'll get infected again. If you need to talk to me, call this land line, okay?"

"Yes sir," Jason said.

"Where are you guys?"

"On our way to Fort Stockton," Jason said. "We had a battle with the Islamists at our first hiding place. Used the phones as bait."

"Really, now?" Chief Ramsey chuckled. "Nice work. How'd you take them on? They must have had you out-gunned."

"My father had a collection of machine guns," Jason said. "We were using BARs against them."

"Well that ought to do it," he said. "So sorry to hear about your parents."

"Thanks," Jason said, feeling the lump back in his throat. "What would you like us to do?"

"Stay in hiding for now, but call this number every few days if you can. Let us know if you find out anything about the enemy."

"I can do that, sir. It's safe to call the land line with my new cellphone, correct?"

"We believe so, yes," Chief Ramsey said.

"Good. I'd better be going."

"Okay, we'll talk again soon. Be careful."

"You too," Jason said. He hung up the phone.

"He have any new instructions?" Carrie asked as they walked out the back door.

"Yeah, call the department land line every couple of days, and stay in hiding," Jason said.

"Do we have to search out a land line for that every time?"

"No, he thinks the cell phones will work as long as we only connect to the land line system at the station. He doesn't trust the cell phones yet."

"They replaced them all, right?"

"Yes, but they haven't figured out how they got hacked, or who did it. They might already be hacked again."

"Oh, geez," Carrie said. She watched as Jason unlocked the coach, then walked up the steps with Chelsea. Dingo was waiting at the door, tail wagging. "Should we take her out?"

"Yeah, I'll do it," Jason said. He grabbed the leash and hooked her up, then headed out for the grassy area on the outside edge of the parking lot. Kyle came out of Kate's trailer. Jason motioned him over.

"You contact work?" Kyle asked.

"Yeah, talked to Chief Ramsey on the land line. We can call that with the cell phones."

"But we can't call the department cellphones yet?"

"Nope," Jason said. "They've been replaced, but the Chief isn't confident that they won't get hacked again."

"Shit, they don't know who did it yet, do they?"

"Nope," Jason said. "Ready to go?"

"Yeah," Kyle said. "Can't wait to hit the sack, man."

"You and me both," Jason said, "but I'm glad we aren't staying here. We don't know if any of the Islamists called in descriptions of our rigs before we killed them."

"Yeah, that thought has crossed my mind. We're visible from that big cross-street over there."

"Yep," Jason said. "See you at the RV Park."

"Later, man," Kyle said.

They saw Curt on the way back to their rigs.

"You pencil necks ready to leave yet?"

"Yeah, Curt, let's blow this joint," Kyle said.

7

Rumors of the Republic

Commissioner Holly rushed into Kip Hendrix's office, terrified look on his face.

"Sorry, sir," Maria said, rushing in behind him. "He wouldn't wait for me to buzz you."

"Don't worry about it, Maria," Hendrix said.

He watched as she left the office, then closed the door behind her.

"Did you hear?" Holly asked, sweat on his brow.

"Calm down," Hendrix said, sitting back down behind his desk. "Did I hear what?"

"Governor Nelson is going to declare Texas a sovereign republic."

"He wouldn't dare," Hendrix said. "Where'd you hear that?"

"One of my contacts on the force. Told me she heard it being discussed by two captain-rank officers."

"I don't believe it," Hendrix said. "How could he get away with that? The administration would nip that in the bud so fast it'd make your head swim."

"You sure about that?" Holly asked.

"Listen to yourself," Hendrix said. "When is this big announcement supposed to take place?"

"Friday," Holly said.

"Care to make a wager?"

"This is serious, dammit," Holly said. "If he does this, we're liable to end up in the gulag. You know that, right?"

Hendrix chuckled. "You really don't understand Nelson, do you?"

"And you do?"

"Yeah, I do," Hendrix said. "You know that we were college buddies, right?"

"I know you went to the same school," Holly said. "Ramsey too, right?"

"Yeah, Ramsey went there too, but I wasn't friends with him. He was from the other side of the tracks. A little too red-neck for my tastes. He *was* tight with Nelson, though. They had some kind of history before they got there."

"You and Nelson obviously had a falling out somewhere along the line, though," Holly said.

"Yeah," Hendrix said, "and I regret it. Probably drank more with that man than anyone else on the planet, and we had some damn good times. I miss being friends with him, and that's the truth. I'd bury the hatchet if he would."

"So we were talking about the gulag," Holly said. "What makes you think he won't clamp down on dissenters if these rumors are true? You think your past friendship will keep you out of trouble?"

Hendrix chuckled. "Nelson believes in the Bill of Rights to a fault. I don't consider that to be a good thing in most situations. Blind obedience to an 18th Century document holds back progress as much as it protects people. But in this case, it'll protect us from getting into trouble with him, unless we do something criminal. That's if he really goes through with this, and I don't think he will."

"Well, whatever you say," Holly said. "You know he shut down the Texas borders, right?"

"Yes, but that's temporary and he had a good reason."

Holly sat back in his chair. "Okay, I'll reserve judgment on the situation."

"We don't even know if we have a *situation*," Hendrix said. "A lot of these rumors turn out to be total BS."

"I had a good source for this one."

"We'll see," Hendrix said. "Now run along. I've got things to do."

"Not finished with the Racing Form yet?" Holly said.

Both of them laughed. "Good, keep the sense of humor. Important during times like this."

"See you later," Holly said. He left the room.

Hendrix leaned back in his chair, watching Holly leave.

"Maria," Kip said.

She rushed in. "Yes, sir."

"Get me Jerry Sutton, please."

"In person or on the phone?" she asked.

He looked her over, dwelling on the way her hips swelled below her waist. She noticed, fidgeting. They made eye contact and Hendrix looked away quickly.

"If he's in the building, have him come here," he said.

"Yes sir," she said, slipping back through the door.

Settle down, dammit. Don't blow it.

"Sir, he's on his way down now," Maria called out.

"Thank you, Maria," he said.

Jerry walked into the suite.

"Go on in," Maria said.

Jerry nodded and walked into Hendrix's office, closing the door behind him.

"What's up, boss?"

"Sit," Hendrix said. "I need you to look into something for me."

"Uh oh, what happened now?" Jerry asked. He sat on the chair facing the desk.

"Holly was just in here telling me that Nelson is about to declare Texas a sovereign republic."

Jerry began to laugh, but stopped when he saw the look on Hendrix's face. "Shit, you aren't kidding, are you?"

"No."

"You don't think DC will let Texas secede, do you?"

"They may have so much on their plate that they can't do anything, at least right away."

"The Feds are holding all the cards. You really think Nelson would take a risk like that?"

"I hope not, but we need to check it out," Hendrix said. "See what you can find out, but keep a low profile, okay?"

"You got it, boss." Sutton got up and left the room.

Hendrix stared at his desk, thinking. "Maria, could you get the Assistant US Attorney General on the line, please?"

"Yes sir," Maria said from her desk.

Kip leaned back in his chair, working out what he would do if Holly was right. Then he got a scared look in his eyes, and leaned forward.

"Maria, forget that last request," Kip said.

"Okay, sir," she said.

8

Stocking and Resting

Kelly drove west on Highway 290, Brenda leaning against the passenger side door, watching the GPS on her new phone.

"I miss having you right next to me," Kelly said.

She glanced at him, then back at her phone. "Oh, all right." She slid over next to him. "Better?"

"Yeah," he said. "We getting close?"

"About three more miles. This is a small park, but there's a bar and grill right next door. We can walk over."

"Good, I could throw back a few before we hit the sack," Kelly said.

"The street view of this place shows it almost deserted. There's only one fifth Wheel in the picture."

"Does it look nice?"

Brenda laughed. "It looks like a piece of pasture on the side of the road with gravel patches. A building in front. Not a lot of amenities, but it looks clean and level."

"I might have to help Junior set up," Kelly said. "He's never had an RV before."

"Where does he live, anyway?"

"In a small place on the edge of what used to be his dad's ranch," Kelly said. "He parceled off and sold all but that one spot. What he has left is actually a decent piece of land. Few acres. Stream running along one side."

"Here it comes," Brenda said. "Make a left turn on Cemetery Road. The park will be on your left."

"That the bar and grill?" Kelly asked, nodding towards a squat-cinder block building with a red metal roof.

"That's it," Brenda said.

Kelly made the left turn half a block past the bar, and then turned left into the park driveway, pulling up in the staging lane. "Damn, this place is packed."

"Sure is," Brenda said. They got out as Junior pulled up behind them, big grin on his face. He bounded out the door of his coach and caught them just outside the office.

"How does she drive?" Kelly asked.

"Like a dream, brother," he said. "That a bar we went past on the way in?"

Brenda snickered. "Figured you'd notice that."

Kelly held the door open for Brenda and Junior.

"Hope you got reservations," the woman behind the desk said. She was middle-aged, dishwater blonde hair, chunky build, remains of a delicately pretty face under the lines.

"I put in a reservation a little while ago," Brenda said. "Under Kelly. Two spaces."

The woman looked at her computer screen. "Oh yeah, the early arrivers. Welcome."

"Thanks," Brenda said.

"Awful busy for mid-week," Kelly said.

"You got *that* right," the woman said as the printer started running behind her.

"Any idea why?" Kelly asked.

The woman slid the printed pages across the counter to Brenda, along with a map of the park. "Been trying to figure that out myself. Things have been a little crazy. There was another riot in Austin last night, and problems in Houston, San Antonio, and Dallas."

"Radio isn't saying much," Junior said. "Had it on most of the way here."

"I know," the woman said. "Same card as you made the reservations with?"

"Yes," Brenda said.

"Okay, then you're all set. Enjoy."

"Thanks," Brenda said.

"Yeah, thanks, baby," Junior said. The woman rolled her eyes as they walked out.

"Geez, Junior, you gonna go hit on that lady?" Kelly asked.

"Like she'd give me the time of day. Look at me. I look like Gabby Hayes."

"If you shaved and got some new clothes, it would help," Brenda said.

"I'll take it under advisement," Junior said.

Kelly laughed. "You haven't changed your look in about thirty years," he said. "C'mon, let's get parked. I'll help you hook up."

"Thanks," Junior said.

Kelly drove into the park, following the map. Their spaces were pull-throughs towards the back. "Hey, this isn't bad at all," he said.

"Better than I expected," Brenda said. "Anything I can help with?"

"You could pretty up the trailer a little," Kelly said. "While I get the utilities hooked up for us and Junior."

"You're gonna show him how, right? So you don't have to do it for him every time?"

"Yeah, that's the plan," Kelly said.

They got out of the truck. Kelly hooked up the trailer utilities quickly, then poked his head in the door.

"Hot in here," Brenda said.

Kelly reached in and flipped the power switch inside the door. "Just turn the thermostat to about 65 and the air conditioner will kick in."

"Okay," she said.

Kelly walked towards the back end of Junior's Brave. He already had the utilities hooked up.

"Wow, you got it done yourself, huh?" Kelly asked.

"The guy at the shop ran me through it," Junior said. "Easy peasy. Think I ought to hook up the sewer?"

"I wouldn't," Kelly said. "We're only gonna overnight here, and our tanks will hold us just fine. When we stop for a few days we'll hook up the rest."

Junior walked to the door of his coach. "Come check it out."

Kelly followed him in and looked around. "Wow, this is nice. Looks like they refurbished everything."

"They did," Junior said. "Like I said, this was a good deal."

"I talked to Hank about it," Kelly said. "He told me he rebuilt the motor himself."

"Who's Hank?"

"The mechanic who did my bearings and tires," Kelly said. "Nice guy."

"The salesman said I ought to get a beater car to tow."

"Not a bad idea," Kelly said. "Find one that's already set up if you can, though. Tow plate setups are pretty damn pricey."

"We going to the bar?"

"I'll check with Brenda. Won't be for very long. I'm beat."

"Yeah," Junior said. "Maybe we ought to take naps and go later."

"That's a better idea," Kelly said. "I'll see you later."

"Later," Junior said.

Kelly walked back to the trailer and went inside. The air was already cooler inside.

"You know, this trailer ain't half bad," Brenda said. "I could live in this for a while. How'd Junior do?"

"He was finished hooking up when I got there," Kelly said. "Salesman went through it with him."

"Well I'll be damned," Brenda said. "He in a hurry to go to the bar?"

"I suggested that we go after we take naps," Kelly said. "Mind?"

"Not even a little bit," she said, yawning. "Let's go to bed."

Kelly nodded and walked to the back where the bed was, stripping off his clothes on the way. He pulled back the covers and got in.

"No hanky panky until we've rested for a while, okay?" Brenda asked. She pulled her blouse over her head. Kelly groaned when he saw her naked chest.

"I'll try," he said. "You're so gorgeous."

"Stop," she said, slipping out of her pants. She climbed into bed next to him. "Should we leave the air conditioner on?"

"Yeah," Kelly said. "It's not the best, and this afternoon will get warm."

"Okay," she said as she snuggled next to him. They were both out in minutes.

Kelly awoke to banging on his door.

"Dammit," he said, picking up his phone.

"What time is it?" Brenda asked, eyes still closed.

"It's 5:30," Kelly said. "Probably Junior wanting to go to the bar. Probably a good time to get up."

She sighed. "You're right. If we get up now, we should be able to sleep at a normal time tonight."

"Yeah," Kelly said, getting out of bed. He slipped on his jeans and looked out the window at Junior's smiling face.

"Time to get up, man," he said, his muffled voice coming through. Kelly cracked open the door.

Robert Boren

"Yeah, you're right," Kelly said. "We'll be out in a few minutes."

"Okay," he said, grinning. He walked back to his rig. Kelly turned to see Brenda pulling her shirt back on.

"Damn, missed it," he said.

"You'll get your chance later," Brenda said. "Wonder if the food is any good at that dive?"

"Only one way to find out," Kelly said, putting his shirt on. They went outside and walked to Junior's coach. He was sitting outside on one of his new folding chairs.

"Nice here," Junior said. "I could get used to this lifestyle."

"You and me both," Kelly said. "Ready?"

"I was born ready," Junior said. Brenda looked at him and chuckled.

"What?" Junior asked.

"Oh, nothing," she said, smiling. "Let's go have a good time."

"Which way? Out the front gate?" Kelly asked.

"No, man, look over there," Junior said. "Northeast corner of the park. There's a break in the fence and a trail. We can walk through right there."

They walked in that direction, going through the opening and onto a dusty dirt path.

"This would be a mess after it rains," Brenda said.

{ 86 }

"Good shortcut for now, though," Kelly said. "Quite a few cars in the parking lot."

They left the dirt path, getting on the black-top parking lot, walking to the door in the front. Kelly held it open for the other two, and they went in.

The bar was along the entire back wall, a doorway into the kitchen to the far left. There were booths along the right and left walls, pool tables in the middle, with a few round cocktail tables filling in the empty space. A juke box played country-western music. People turned to look at the trio as they walked in.

"No space at the bar," Junior said.

"Rather sit at a booth anyway," Brenda said. She pointed to an empty booth half way down on the left side. "How's that one?"

"Looks good to me," Kelly said. They made their way over and sat down. A pretty young bar maid came over and stood at the end of the table, smiling at them. She had dark brown hair, long and straight, brilliant eyes and an innocent smile. A nose ring in her right nostril gave her a wilder look that she would have had otherwise.

"What can I get for y'all?" she asked in a West Texas drawl.

"Got any IPA on tap?" Kelly asked.

"Sure do. Local brew, best in the state," she said.

"I'll take that."

"White wine," Brenda said. "Any kind will do."

"And for you, sir?" she asked, looking at Junior.

"Got Bud Lite on draft?" he asked.

"Sure do," she said.

"Good, rinse me a mug with that swill and then fill it with IPA," he said. Kelly laughed out loud, Brenda shook her head, and the waitress wasn't sure what to say.

"He's just kidding, honey," Brenda said. "Take it from a fellow barmaid."

"Oh, you know the business?" she asked. "Need a job? We're looking for somebody to help out."

"I own my own place in Dripping Springs," Brenda said. "On vacation."

"Yeah, an extended vacation," Junior said. "I'm available for beer tasting. Oh, and I'd be happy to interview potential bar maids, too."

Kelly laughed again.

"Oh, brother," Brenda said. The barmaid giggled. "I guess I'll have to ask the boss about that."

"You have food?" Brenda asked.

"Yeah, but the choices are a little limited. Ran out of a lot of stuff. We didn't expect this many people here mid-week. Not sure what's up with that."

"Well, bring us menus and tell us what you have left," Brenda said.

"Okay," she said. "Drinks coming right up."

She walked away, hips swaying in her tight jeans.

"That's a fine piece of woman-flesh," Junior said.

"Yeah, who's old enough to be your granddaughter, you old reprobate," Brenda quipped.

Junior chuckled. Kelly shook his head.

"Wish they had the TV going in here," Brenda said. "Love to know what the hell is going on with all these travelers."

"I got a TV in my rig," Junior said. "We can check it out when we get back if you want."

"Get anything over antenna out here?" Kelly asked. "They didn't have cable."

"Don't know. Haven't checked it out yet."

"How'd you sleep in your new rig?" Brenda asked.

"Like a baby," he said. "I wouldn't have woken up, but I set the alarm on my phone. Didn't want to get my hours all messed up."

"I wasn't so happy when you banged on the door," Kelly said. "But I'm glad you did."

"Me too," Brenda said.

"Here you go," the barmaid said, carrying a tray with drinks over. She handed them out, and slipped them the menus.

"We're out of beef," she said. "Still got chicken, catfish, and turkey burgers."

"Thanks," Brenda said, looking at the menu.

"Oh, and I asked the owner about your offer," she said, looking at Junior. "He almost fell on the floor laughing. That was good. He's had a rough few days."

"Sorry to hear it," Junior said. "What happened?"

"His kid brother got killed on Falcon Lake a couple days ago."

"No," Kelly said. "Tell him we're sorry."

"Tell him we'll kill a few Islamists for him," Junior said, eyes narrowing.

"Kill?" the barmaid asked, frightened.

"Don't worry," Brenda said. "He's not as crazy as he looks. You see the Dripping Springs attack on TV? And the battle in Austin a couple days ago?"

"Yes," she said. "Just awful."

"These two were in the group of men who did the counter attacks. That's why we're on the road."

Her eyes got wide. "No, really?"

"Really," Brenda said.

"You've seen some action yourself," Kelly said to Brenda. "Saved my ass at the bar, remember?"

She smiled. "Anyway, they've got our number, so we had to leave."

"Casey might want to talk to you guys," she said. "You mind?"

"Casey?" Kelly asked.

"The owner," she said, smiling. "He almost shut this place down to go after them. Business took off so fast that he gave up on that idea."

A man rushed in the door of the bar. "Hey, something big happened in San Antonio!" he yelled.

"What?" asked a man sitting by the door.

"Damn Islamists stormed city hall. Killed the mayor and half the city council. There's a big gun battle going on there now."

"Somebody turn on that TV," another man said.

The bar maid rushed over to the bar, grabbed the remote, and turned on the TV. Video of downtown San Antonio came on the screen. The announcer came on.

"We can confirm that the mayor and all city council members who were in today have been killed, their headless bodies dumped off the roof onto the lawn below. Police and armed citizens have the building surrounded."

"Holy shit," Junior said. "Too bad we're so far away from there."

"I'm glad," Brenda said. "Look at all those citizens. They outnumber the police, from the look of it."

"This attack follows similar attacks earlier today in Houston and Dallas. This is the only attack where

the terrorists were successful at getting inside the city headquarters."

"Well, now we know what's going on," Kelly said. "Damn cretins."

"We'll meet them again," Junior said. "They won't enjoy it."

A large man walked towards the booth, white apron on, followed by the bar maid. He had long hair in a net, clean shaven, with muscular shoulders and arms.

"This is them," the barmaid said.

"Thanks, Darby," he said. "Hi folks. Darby told me who you were. Nice to meet you, and kudos for your actions."

"Thanks. I'm Kelly. This is Brenda, and the crazy one there is Junior. Good to meet you. Sorry to hear about your brother."

He nodded, grim look on his face. "I'm Casey," he said. "You guys are on the lam?"

"Yeah, we're hoping to meet up with the rest of our group out west."

"What will you do then?" Casey asked.

"Regroup and plan attacks," Kelly said.

"The rest of your group took off too?"

"Yeah, after we found out how we were being tracked," Junior said. "Hey, you talked to any officials on your cell phone?"

"Yeah," he said. "Why?"

"Do you know if you were talking to them on a land line, or on a cell line?" Kelly asked, eyes darting around the room.

"I don't know," Casey said. "Why?"

"Islamists hacked the Austin PD cell phones, and put in a back door through the encryption. It was like a virus, and replicated onto any other cell phones making contact with them."

"Oh, crap," Casey said. "I'd better find out about that."

"What kind of cell phone do you have?" Kelly asked.

"Android," he said.

"Yank the battery, and call the authorities you talked to on your land line. They can't trace that."

"This is how they found that Austin cop's parents, isn't it?" Casey asked.

"Yeah," Kelly said. "They also found all of us, the night after the Dripping Springs Superstore attack."

"They kill any of your men?"

Junior chuckled. "Nope, but we killed a lot of them."

"No shit," Casey said. "How many?"

"Eighty or ninety that night," Kelly said. "Hundred more in Austin the following day. Oh, and this started with about forty at the Superstore, but we didn't do all of them."

"They're still after you, then?"

"Oh, yeah," Kelly said, "but we dumped the phones. Put them on a freight train to Newark. I don't think the enemy knows where we are."

Casey laughed. "Good."

"Yeah," Junior said. "You might have somebody on your tail. I'd watch yourself. Check on that phone problem. Get rid of your phone if there's any chance they've hacked it."

"Thanks for that info," he said. "I'll go yank the battery now."

"No problema," Junior said.

"Food and drinks on the house for you guys tonight," Casey said.

"You don't have to do that," Brenda said.

"I want to," he said. "How long you gonna be here?"

"Only overnight," Kelly said.

"Well, good luck to you guys." He walked back to the kitchen.

"We'd better watch ourselves," Junior said. "There might be some action here. You got your piece?"

"Yeah," Kelly said.

"Me too, in my purse," Brenda said.

The barmaid came over. "You guys decide what you want to eat?"

"Yeah," Brenda said. The barmaid took their orders and walked away.

"Hey, look at the TV screen!" Junior said.

Kelly turned towards it and laughed out loud. "No way."

"What?" Brenda asked. She looked at the TV. "Hey, is that our boxcar?"

The screen showed a derailed train, one of the boxcars a twisted wreck. The banner said "TRAIN DERAILMENT OUTSIDE NEWARK, NEW JERSEY."

9

Forest Assault

E ric showed Kim how to fire the AK-47, then unhitched the Bronco from the back of his Class C.

"The guns are loaded," she said. "What else do we need?"

"Both sets of binoculars," Eric said. "I've got two sleeping bags in the back. I'll toss them in the back just in case."

"Okay, I'll get some food too, and some toilet paper."

"Good," he said. "Paco, come here."

The dog trotted over and jumped into the Bronco. The couple got the rest of their supplies loaded and then locked up the rig.

"Ready?" Eric asked.

"Yeah," Kim said. "Let's go." Eric backed the Bronco up and drove towards the road, turning onto it and speeding up.

"Keep your eyes open," he said. "Let me know if you see anybody."

"Will do," she said. "How capable is this off-road?"

"It's tricked out for racing," Eric said.

"Did you race?"

"A little," he said. "Was costing me too much money. I know how to drive, though. I'll outrun just about anything with this sucker out in the dirt."

"Good," Kim said.

They drove down the long straight road at a good clip, making time they could only dream of in the motor home.

"See that road up there?" Eric asked. "That's Oilfield Road."

"Which way should we turn?"

"We were gonna go left, to pick up that state road," Eric said. "Might as well see if the coast is clear that way."

He made the left turn onto the road, which was still dirt, but better maintained. He sped up.

"More tree farms, and more of those asphalt patches," Kim said.

"Yeah," Eric said. "Look, mud ahead. I'll check for tracks. Ought to be able to tell if a bunch of trucks came through recently."

He stopped in front of a low spot in the road went out to look.

There were many imprints of dual tires.

"They went this way all right," Eric said to Kim as she looked.

"I wonder how far away they are?"

"Probably not very, since we've been moving so fast," Eric said, looking down the road. "We need to be careful."

"Let's go," Kim said.

They got back into the Bronco and took off, going slower. As they got near the crest of a small hill, gunfire erupted in front of them.

"Shit!" Kim said.

"Don't worry, they aren't shooting at us," Eric said. "See that hill there, where the road goes up and we can't see past? I'll pull over into the brush before we get there, and we'll take a look."

Kim nodded and Eric pulled in, driving behind the wall of forest on the side of the road. "Look, there's a bluff up ahead. I'll bet we can see what's going on from there. Maybe even take a couple of pot shots."

Kim glanced at him, scared to death as Eric drove up towards the bluff, parking well out of sight from the road. They got out, Eric grabbing the 30-30 and an AK-47, Kim grabbing the other AK-47.

"Quietly," Eric whispered.

"What about Paco?"

"Maybe we ought to bring him just in case," Eric said. He opened the back of the Bronco and motioned. Paco leapt out, getting next to him, tail wagging.

Another gunshot went off. Then two more.

Eric and Kim hurried up the hill and got on their bellies, inching forward. There were three troop transport trucks stopped on the road, and Islamists were in a line facing some citizens. Several citizens lay dead on the ground. One of the Islamists was yelling at the first citizen in the line-up. The citizen flipped him the bird, so the Islamist got back and nodded to the others. They fired, killing the man.

"No!" Kim whispered.

"Think you can hit them from here?" Eric whispered.

"I don't know," she whispered. "Can you?"

"Yeah, they're close enough for the AKs. If there were less of them I'd use the 30-30. Better sights."

"They're about to kill another one," Kim whispered.

Eric aimed the AK-47 at the person yelling at the next citizen and pulled the trigger. The Islamist flew to the ground, and the others looked around in a panic. The citizens took off running.

"Blast them," Eric said as he opened up, firing as quickly as he could. Kim joined him. They killed several Islamists as they scurried for cover. The Islamists tried to fight back, firing wildly from behind the trucks.

"Shoot their truck tires," Eric said.

Kim nodded and the both aimed at them, hitting all but the first truck, which was starting to roll. Suddenly more gunfire hit the truck from the right side of road below. The truck rolled to the ditch, somebody yelling in Arabic. Several men in camo hunting gear ran into view, shooting at the remaining trucks.

"Good guys!" Kim whispered, grinning at Eric.

"The enemy has cover behind those trucks," Eric said. "I think I can get on the other side of them if I'm quick about it, while they're fighting with the hunters."

"I'm going too," Kim said. Eric looked at her and nodded. They took off down the bluff as quickly as they could, Paco trying to keep up. The hunters continued to fire at the Islamists on the far said of the trucks, pinning them down, but they couldn't move forward any further without getting hit.

"Almost there," Eric whispered as he and Kim sprinted to the far side of the road. "Get ready to hit the dirt and open fire."

They got on the other side of the road and rolled into the ditch, opening fire on the hiding Islamists. They screamed with panic, not even trying to return fire, running forward where the hunters could see them. The hunters opened up, killing all but one of them, who threw down his weapons and held up his hands. Eric stood up and waved, getting the attention of one of the hunters.

"American!" Eric shouted.

"Come forward, but keep your guns down," yelled the man walking up to the live Islamist. Eric and Kim hurried over as the hunter was questioning the Islamist.

"Where were you heading?"

The Islamist looked at him blankly.

"Don't think he can speak English, Dirk," said small, round man next to him.

"How'd you like me to shoot you in the balls?" Dirk asked. The Islamist got a terrified look on his face.

"He understands all right," Dirk said. He was a small man with a scrappy look and piercing eyes, red haired with a heavy beard.

"You gonna talk?" he asked.

The Islamist stood still silently, trembling.

"We don't have time for this crap," Dirk said. He pulled out a big bowie knife and slit the man's throat.

Kim screamed. Eric looked at her and shook his head no.

"Where'd you folks come from?" Dirk asked, walking over. "Sorry about that. Didn't want to waste another bullet."

"Friends of these guys beheaded my parents a couple days ago," Eric said. "I'm not exactly on their side."

"Neither am I," Kim said. "Sorry, that was just more gruesome than I'm used to seeing."

"Where'd you get the AKs?" Dirk asked.

"We were being followed by a truck full of these guys in northwestern Louisiana," Eric said. "We got the drop on them just past Longstreet. Blew them away, took their weapons."

"Do tell," Dirk said. "What's your name?"

"Eric Finley," he said. "This is Kim."

"Good to know you guys," Dirk said, "I'm Dirk. This chubby little guy here is Chance. The tall skinny guy next to him is Kenny, and the big guy next to him is Don."

"Nice to meet you guys," Eric said. "We saw two groups of these trucks go by this morning. The first was a group of eight. The second was a group of twelve."

"Dammit," Dirk said. "How long ago?"

"Less than an hour," Eric said. "We should keep our eyes open. Possible they heard the battle."

"Yeah," Dirk said, eyes darting around. "Also possible some more might drive right up here."

"Who were those people they were executing?" Kim asked.

"The Hadley family and some of their farm hands," Dirk said. "Good people. This just makes me sick."

"Looks like some of them got away at least."

"Yeah, but the old man and his sons all bought it," Chance said. "That's the end of their operation."

"What are you guys doing out here, anyway?" Dirk asked.

"I was coming home from Florida to bury my dad," Eric said. "Got turned away at the border east of Houston, so I went north past the river and snuck over from the area west of Longstreet. I'm trying to meet up with my brother."

"Your last name sounds familiar," Don said.

"My brother was one of the Austin cops who was involved in the Dripping Springs attack," Eric said.

"Oh, shit, I know who that is," Chance said. "Saw the story on TV. Your brother and his partner are in hiding."

"Yep," Eric said. "A long way off. We're trying to get to Carthage so we can pick up Highway 79 and head into the Austin area."

"You can get there through Deadwood via State Road 3359," Chance said. "At least that state road is paved."

"Can you guys contact somebody about these folks coming in?" Kim asked.

"Yeah," Dirk said. "Lucky we happened upon these guys. First time we've seen anything like this around here."

"How much trouble could they cause in Deadwood or Carthage?"

"Well, we're from Deadwood," Chance said. "Just over a hundred of us living there. It could be bad."

"Yeah, if they saw twenty trucks go by, we might have a big problem," Dirk said. "Don, call your brother, and then we'd better saddle up."

"Brother?" Kim asked.

"He's the town constable," Dirk said.

"Maybe we ought to go with you guys," Eric said. "We'll help you fight them."

"I'd appreciate it," Dirk said, "but no pressure."

"Hey, we got to drive a motor home through there. I'd rather take out the problem before we try that."

Dirk chuckled. "Good point. Let's go. Our trucks are down about a hundred yards. What are you in? You'll have to get around these trucks. The ground is a little soft."

"Old Bronco," Eric said. "We won't have a problem."

"Good, see you in a few minutes," Dirk said.

"Hey, grab their guns," Chance said.

"Yeah, good idea," Kenny said. "I know how to fire those."

"No answer from my brother," Don said, concerned look on his face.

"Shit," Dirk said. "Let's step it up."

The men gathered up the AKs and ammo and trotted forward on the road, getting into a pickup truck and a Jeep over the bluff.

"Let's go," Eric said. He and Kim rushed back to the Bronco with Paco and got on the road, going around the trucks and following Dirk and his men. They raced down Oilfield Road, going almost too fast, vehicles bouncing around violently.

"This is scary," Kim said, holding onto the sides of her seat.

"Yeah, sorry," Eric said. "We're liable to run into a pretty good sized battle up here. Be ready to high-tail it back to the Bronco. There's other ways we can get to Carthage."

"I think you were right about taking out those guys before we take the motor home through here," Kim said.

"They're turning left," Eric said.

"State Road 3359," Kim said. "Good, it *is* paved."

They three vehicles sped up to about sixty miles per hour.

"How much further?" Kim asked.

"Not very," Eric said. "Look, they're already slowing down."

"Road changed to 2517," Kim said.

"Yeah, as I remember there's one more turn. To the right."

They drove for about five minutes, and saw Dirk's men veer right.

"There they go," Kim said. "State Road 4468."

"Yeah," Eric said. "This dumps onto the main road through town."

"Hope they haven't set up an ambush," Kim said.

"You and me both," Eric said.

"They're turning right again," Kim said.

"Yeah, right before this dead-ends into the main drag." He took the turn, leading to an asphalt patch. "Another old oil well."

Dirk's truck and the Jeep parked. Eric parked the Bronco right next to them, and everybody got out.

"Figured we'd better walk the rest of the way and check it out," Dirk said.

"Smart," Eric said. "Checked out on those AKs?"

"Yeah," Don said. "They had a lot of ammo. We didn't even bring all of it with us."

"If we survive this, we'll help you guys tow those trucks out of the way," Chance said. "Probably can't get around them with a motor home."

"More enemy trucks will have a problem too," Eric said. "That's a good thing for us at the moment."

"You think there's more coming?" Chance asked.

"Better than even chance," Eric said. "I wonder how many groups went through before we saw these."

"Yeah, tell me about it," Dirk said.

"Hey, just got a text from my brother," Don said. "The enemy is in town. Killed a few people when they arrived. They're at the store getting supplies now. The town's people are getting ready to assault them."

"Good, you tell him we're coming?"

"Yeah," Don said. "We'd better haul ass."

They picked up their weapons and ammo and trotted through the forest towards town.

"Look," Dirk whispered. "Trucks at the gas station."

Gunfire started up, sounding like it was a few hundred yards ahead of them.

"My brother and the others just attacked the store," Don whispered.

"Let's hit those trucks," Chance said.

Dirk nodded, and they got into position. "Fire at will," Dirk said. "Watch your ammo."

They opened up, hitting the men re-fueling the trucks, and shooting the tires out. A couple of the Islamists took off running. Eric popped up and sprinted towards them as Paco followed, killing both before they got thirty yards.

"Damn, he's fast," Chance said. "C'mon, let's get into town."

They ran forward. The other trucks were parked ahead of them. An Islamist in back of one saw Eric running towards them and tried to shoot, but he got hit square in the face before he could fire his weapon.

"Looks like some of the trucks are backed up at the loading dock behind the store," Dirk said. "Let's stop them before they can take off."

"I got an idea," Eric said. "C'mon, Kim."

They sprinted towards a truck and jumped into the cab.

"Yes! The keys are in it," Eric said. He started the engine, and they drove forward, pulling into the narrow driveway to the loading dock. "Got them bottled up now!"

Somebody opened fire as they were heading for the back of the truck.

"Get down!" Eric said. Kim went under the truck and crawled to the back as Eric opened fire, dropping an Islamist who was standing on the loading dock. He was replaced by several more, all of whom opened fire at Eric. He dived under the truck and came out the back side. Kim was in the back end of the truck, looking at a wooden crate.

"Hey, grenades," she whispered. Eric got a grin on his face and opened the box.

"Holy shit," he said. "Think you can cover me while I toss a couple of these?"

"Yeah," she said. "Let's hurry before more of them show up."

Eric grabbed two of the grenades, and they snuck alongside the truck. Paco growled. Eric whipped around and shot a fighter who was sneaking up on them. Then more shots came from the loading dock. There were five Islamists there. Kim opened up from behind the front tire, lying on the ground. They took cover, and Eric threw a grenade. It rolled under the first truck and blew up, a huge fireball filling the area. Two of the Islamists screamed, diving off the dock on fire. Kim shot both of them while Eric threw the other grenade, blowing up the other truck.

"Shoot the tires in this truck and let's get away from here," Eric said. "I'm grabbing more grenades."

Kim nodded, shooting the tires in the front. Another Islamist opened fire from the loading dock. Eric nailed him. "Maybe I should try to toss a grenade or two right into that loading dock."

"Be careful," Kim said.

"Cover me," he said, rushing back to the box. He grabbed several more grenades, and then jumped up above the retaining wall of the driveway, sprinting down towards the loading dock as Kim continued to fire. He tossed a grenade into the loading dock, where he saw five men standing. It went off as they tried to run, blowing parts of them all over the place. Eric followed with another grenade, which rolled into the back door of the store, blowing up, men screaming inside and yelling in Arabic.

Kim joined Eric behind the driveway. "The others just went in the front of the store. Maybe we should bring some more grenades over there and help them out."

"Yeah," Eric said. They sprinted to the back of the truck, grabbing several more grenades and rushing to the front of the store. Dirk was lying on the sidewalk in front of the windows, pinned down by fire coming from inside. Eric got his attention and held up a grenade. Dirk smiled and nodded.

"What should we do?" Kim asked.

"Shoot out the window and I'll toss one in," Eric said.

"Okay," she said. Eric crawled closer as Kim opened fire. Islamists opened up through the window at her, firing wide. Eric tossed a grenade in, and a swirl of glass and fire blasted out. Dirk put his hands over his head and curled up, trying to avoid the storm of fragments.

Eric tossed a second one in, and it blew up further in the store. Then Dirk got up and ran through the broken window, firing madly, Arabic screams coming from the inside. Eric sprinted in and joined him, followed by Don and Chance. Kim kept watch outside with Paco. After a few minutes there was silence.

The men came out, tired, carrying their weapons.

"Everybody okay?" Kim asked.

"Kenny," Dirk said, breaking down. "He got killed right at the beginning."

"Keep your guards up, guys," Eric said. "There weren't enough trucks here. Remember that Kim and I saw twenty drive down the road. We stopped three in that first battle. There was six at the gas station, all disabled now, and three here. That leaves eight. Any idea where they might be?"

"If they're close enough to hear this, they might be here any second," Chance said.

"Where'd you get the grenades?" Dirk asked.

"That truck that we used to bottle up the driveway into the loading dock," Kim said. "Big wooden crate of them in the back."

"We'd better check all the trucks," Don said. "I'll bet there's a lot of stuff we can use."

A group of men ran forward. Don turned towards them and smiled.

"Hey, brother," he said. A large older gentleman rushed over and hugged him.

"Nobody got killed?" Dirk asked.

"Nope," the man said.

"We lost Kenny," Dirk said.

"Oh, God no," he said, eyes squinting. Tears ran down his cheeks.

Don hugged him again, then turned towards Eric and Kim. "This is Francis, my brother. Town Constable."

"I'm Eric, and this is Kim," Eric said. "You see other trucks?"

"Yeah," Francis said, trying to calm down. "We wasted five of them on the far end of town. That's why we weren't here when you guys showed up. Three trucks got away. I already called Carthage.

They're setting up a nice welcome, and they have a lot more people than we do."

"Thank God," Kim said.

"Where you folks from?" Francis asked.

"Florida, but I'm a Texas native," Eric said. "We were coming home to bury my parents and take revenge on the Islamists who beheaded them in Fredericksburg."

"Oh, shit, you're related to that Austin cop," Francis said, stepping forward to shake his hand.

"Brothers," Eric said.

"You going to join him?" Francis asked.

"Yeah, if I can find him," Eric said. "They're headed for West Texas."

"Well, I'm glad you guys showed up when you did," Dirk said.

"Me too," Eric said. "I think we'd better get our motor home and high-tail it out of here before more of these cretins come along."

"If they haven't already," Kim said.

"We'll follow you back," Dirk said. "Hey, Francis, think you could follow us with a couple of your tow trucks?"

"Sure," he said. "Why?"

"There's three of these troop transport trucks blocking the road back there."

"Yeah," Francis said. "Let's go."

"Mind if we take some of those grenades?" Eric asked.

"Hey, finders' keepers," Dirk said. "We'll check the other trucks. There's probably more."

"Yeah," Don said. "We'd better go. I have a feeling there's more of these folks coming. We might want to set up a roadblock."

"Just thinking that," Francis said.

"All right, guys, see you soon." Eric said. He and Kim walked by the back of the truck. They picked up the rest of the grenades and hurried to the Bronco, Paco following them.

"I like those guys," Eric said.

"Me too." Kim got into the Bronco and patted her lap. Paco jumped up, and she shut the door as Eric backed out. They headed back to the trucks.

"Still there," Eric said. "Half expected to find more Islamists trying to clear them out of the way."

"I know," she said. They slowed down, Eric looking around, trying to see an ambush. Nobody was around so they drove around the trucks.

"Go slow when we get near the crest of the hill," Kim said, looking ahead nervously.

"Yeah," Eric said. He slowed to a stop. "I'm gonna peek over."

"I'll go too." They grabbed their weapons and moved up, crawling on their bellies to look over.

"Nobody I can see," Eric said.

"Nope, thank God," Kim said. She looked over to the side and saw a rock the size of a basketball. "Let's roll that down the hill."

Eric looked at her and grinned. "Yeah, let's do that." They moved over to it and rolled the heavy rock to the crest of the hill, pushing it over. It rolled down. Nothing. "I think we're safe. Let's go."

They ran back to the Bronco and got in, heading over the crest and down the road, making the right turn back onto the small dirt road. The coach was undisturbed. Eric drove behind it, then got out and hitched up the Bronco as Kim took Paco into the motor home. Eric got in and they rolled down to the road slowly. Then they took off, Eric's eyes darting between the rear view mirrors and the road in front of him every few seconds.

"You look really nervous," Kim said.

"Damn straight," Eric said. "We should have asked those guys to call Longstreet. Hope the Islamists didn't kill everybody there."

"Yeah, me too," Kim said. "Think we're going to make it?"

"Probably, but we got some rough times coming."

Kim watched him for a moment. "Wonder how it's going for your brother? Wish we still had phones."

"Here comes Oilfield road," Eric said, making the left turn. They sped up, but had to hold it under forty miles per hour.

"Think they got the road cleared yet?" Kim asked.

"We'll see," Eric said. "Hope the folks in Carthage took out those last three truckloads."

"How big is Carthage?"

"A lot bigger than Deadwood," Eric said.

Kim laughed. "I wouldn't even call Deadwood a town. It's a wide spot in the road with a few stores."

Eric chuckled. "Yeah, that's about it."

"Here comes that bluff again. Think we ought to stop and take a look?"

"Nah, we know nobody came through since we got the coach moving, and we know where those last three trucks went," Eric said.

"There's no other ways here?" Kim asked.

"I don't think so," Eric said. "Now you've got me nervous." He stopped the coach, and they got out and rushed to the crest of the hill. They peered over. Dirk and his men were down there. The three trucks were out of the road, and they were busy moving supplies from them into their vehicles.

"Maybe we shouldn't have shot the tires," Kim said as they drove down the hill.

"Yeah, maybe," Eric said. "If they want the trucks, they could fix the tires easy enough." He rolled to a stop, and Dirk trotted over.

"Thanks," Eric said.

"Don't mention it," Dirk said. "No problems between where your rig was and here, I take it."

"None," Eric said. "I was thinking. You guys might want to call Longstreet. Warn them about this traffic. I'd do it myself, but we had to ditch our cell phones."

"Yeah, that's a good idea. I'll pass it along to Francis."

"Good. Any word on those last three trucks?"

"Yeah, the police in Carthage captured them without a fight. There were thirty enemy fighters in those trucks. They're all in jail now."

"What are you guys gonna do?" Eric asked.

"The Army National Guard is sending a detachment down here to set up some roadblocks," Dirk said. "They see four different routes that could be a problem. We'll help them set up, and then hopefully go back to a normal life."

"Good luck with that," Eric said. "Maybe you guys are remote enough to avoid any more problems."

"Yeah, hopefully," Dirk said. "The cities are a mess. Heard what happened earlier today?"

"No," Eric said.

"Attacks in Houston, Dallas, and San Antonio," he said. "Citizens and the local police put them down quickly, everywhere except San Antonio."

"What happened there?" Kim asked.

"The enemy got into city hall. Killed the mayor and all the city councilmen who were there. They got a standoff going right now, with hostages."

"Dammit," Eric said.

"The only good news there was outside. Citizens and police killed over a hundred enemy fighters in the downtown area."

"Good," Kim said.

"We'd better take off," Eric said. "Thanks again for your help."

"No, thank you," Dirk said, reaching inside to shake hands. "Maybe we'll meet again someday."

"Wouldn't surprise me," Eric said. "Take care of yourself."

"You too," he said, stepping back from the rig. Eric drove forward, waving to the men by the trucks.

"It's going to get dark in a few hours," Kim said. "We might have to spend another night out here in the boonies."

"Hope not," Eric said. "Let's see what time it is when we get to Carthage. That town is large enough to be safe."

10

OPEC Creek

The sleek boat cut through the water, the buzz of the engine breaking the calm.

"There it is, dude," Juan Carlos said, pointing at the makeshift docks and temporary buildings at OPEC Creek.

"See it," Brendan said. "Look, men coming onto the docks."

"Yeah." Juan Carlos slowed the boat as he approached, men rushing over to assist.

"Where's the rest of the boats?" Brendan asked.

"I hope they're out on patrol," Juan Carlos said.

"Yeah, that'd be better than on the bottom," Brendan said as he tossed the bowline to one of the men. He rushed to the stern line and tossed that to another man as Juan Carlos shut off the engine.

"Glad to see you guys," a man walking up said. "I'm Lieutenant Richardson." He was a man of medium build with freckles and red hair. "Heard you guys have a fuel-line problem."

"Yeah," Juan Carlos said. "Bullet hit the armor on the transom and bounced back. Nicked the main fuel feeder line. See?"

Lieutenant Richardson got closer and looked, seeing the oily sheen on the water in the mid-morning sunshine. "You got here just in time. This leaked a little."

"Not surprised," Juan Carlos said. He stepped off the boat. "You know about Chauncey, right?" he asked, pointing at his body on the deck.

"Yeah, we heard," he said. "Sorry."

"How many did we lose at Zapata?" Brendan asked.

"Too many. You guys need more ammo, I suspect," Lieutenant Richardson said.

"Yeah, more .50 cal," Juan Carlos said. "I don't suppose you got any more rockets for the SMAW?"

"No," he said. "Where the hell did you get that thing?"

"Chauncey brought it," Juan Carlos said. "He got it from the DPS Director."

"Wallis, eh," Lieutenant Richardson said. "He's missing."

"You mean missing from the attack at Zapata?" Brendan asked.

"No, before that. Just disappeared. Heard rumors about the Feds being after him."

"Who's in command here?" Brendan asked.

"Captain Jefferson," he said. "He's waiting to talk with you. We've had a Major General from the National Guard here too. Not sure if he still is."

"Gallagher?" Juan Carlos asked.

"Yeah, that's him. You know him?"

"Met him at Zapata," Juan Carlos said.

"You better get in there," Lieutenant Richardson said. "Furthest building."

"Okay," Juan Carlos said.

Brendan joined him, and they left the dock, walking on the dirt path to the buildings.

"This is messed up, dude," Juan Carlos said. "Hope Wallis is okay."

"He's probably just in hiding," Brendan said.

"If that was true, wouldn't Gallagher be missing too?"

"Good point, man," Brendan said. He pushed the door to the third building open and held it for Juan Carlos. Captain Jefferson saw them right away and motioned them over.

"Good job, men," he said. "So sorry to hear about Chauncey. How'd he get it?"

"Snipers on the cliffs," Brendan said.

"Shit," Jefferson said. "That hurt. Can't afford to lose men like him. Let's go in the conference room, okay?"

"Okay," Juan Carlos said.

Jefferson lead them to a door and held it open for them. Major General Gallagher was sitting at the far end of the table.

"Good to see you men again," he said. "Sorry about Chauncey."

Juan Carlos and Brendan nodded and sat. Captain Jefferson sat across the table from them.

"What the hell happened at Zapata?" Brendan asked.

"Venezuelan Air Force, flying Russian attack helicopters low enough to stay off the radar," Gallagher said. "Got in and out before we could do anything."

"How many did we lose?" Juan Carlos asked.

"About half the men there," Jefferson said. "Luckily none of the boats were there when they hit us. They were all out on the lake."

"We lose any other boats?" Brendan asked.

"Yeah," Jefferson said. "Four, two sunk by cutters, two hit by those choppers when they were on their way to Zapata."

"What's going on with our air power?" Juan Carlos asked.

"Yesterday they were in the west, over Mexico," Gallagher said, "helping along the California and Arizona border. We have a bigger problem there than we do here."

"You talking the US Airforce or the Texas Air National Guard?" Brendan asked.

"Both. Don't worry, we'll get them back soon enough," Gallagher said. "If we don't stop the invasion in California and Arizona, we could lose the entire southwest. I know it's tough for us, but we'll survive."

"How?" Brendan asked. "If they're flying choppers at us, we *won't* survive."

"We took care of the chopper situation," Gallagher said. "Their base in northern Mexico was hit last night. They won't have more until they can get them from Venezuela, and we're making that a lot tougher."

"I thought you just said we didn't have our air power," Juan Carlos said.

"Calm down," Jefferson said.

"No, I don't blame him," Gallagher said. "The enemy choppers were based just south of Arizona. Our birds hit their base on the way west. Hit them again on the way home."

"Where's Director Wallis?" Brendan asked.

"Safe," Gallagher said. "This doesn't leave the room. He's in a secure location along with other key people, ahead of the Governor's announcement in a couple of days."

"What announcement?" Brendan asked.

"Governor Nelson is declaring Texas to be a sovereign nation," Gallagher said. "We alluded to this possibility in the last meeting, remember?"

"Yeah, I remember," Juan Carlos said. "This isn't making sense to me. Not at all. Every time we think we're gonna get air support, we end up holding the bag on our own."

"Juan Carlos," Jefferson said. Gallagher put his hands up.

"I want to hear his concerns," he said. "We're in the fog of war. The situation has been changing by the hour. Last night I had no idea we would send our air force to help with the situation in California and Arizona. The entire southern border is like a big leaky dike, and we don't have enough fingers to plug all the holes at the same time. If a hole gets bigger all of a sudden, we rush help over there. That's what has been going on. Believe it or not, this stretch here along Falcon Lake is the best protected section of border we've got. You can't walk it, and it's too wide to swim across. We've taken some awful casualties here, but we're gonna turn the corner soon. Trust me on that."

"How do we get more SMAW rockets?" Brendan asked. "We asked for re-supply on the dock, and the lieutenant had no idea what we were talking about."

"Chauncey was piloting those on the QT, working with Wallis," Gallagher said. "They obviously make a difference, but we've been keeping it close to the vest. They were beyond what we got approval for from the Texas Senate, but that situation was rectified yesterday." He paused and smiled. "Follow me. I want to show you something." He led the men out of the conference room and down the hall, into another room. Gallagher switched on the lights and motioned them in.

Brendan gasped when he saw what was in there.

Juan Carlos laughed. "Bitchen, dude."

There were several rows of automatic rocket launchers and gimbal assemblies stacked against the back wall.

"We're going to mount these on the boats, aren't we?" Brendan asked.

"Yeah," Jefferson said. "After the briefing from Chauncey on the first attack run, it became pretty obvious that we needed a hands-free stabilized solution, controlled by the boat's pilot. Here it is. We'll be making an announcement about these in about four hours. They'll be installed over the next three days. You guys get the first one."

"Excellent," Brendan said. "We get to keep the hand-held SMAW too, right?"

"I suppose so," Jefferson said. "Why would you want that?"

"We were just forced onto the beach, remember?" Brendan said. "We got lucky and were able to fix the problem with our boat. If we hadn't been, the SMAW would have helped a lot."

"We still have the others that Wallis got?" Gallagher asked.

"They were at Zapata," Jefferson said. "I'll make sure they're brought here if they survived, along with any rockets that are left. I'll let you know if we need more."

"Good, you do that," Gallagher said. "Men, any more questions?"

"Nope," they said.

"Okay, get some grub and rest. We'll have the meeting about the new hardware in a few hours."

"Thank you, sir," Juan Carlos said.

"Yes, thank you, sir," Brendan said. They left the storage room with Captain Jefferson.

"Remember what he said. Mum's the word until the meeting." Jefferson said.

"Yeah, we get it," Brendan said.

"No problema," Juan Carlos said.

They walked to the first building to get some food.

11

Sonora

Jason was tired of the drive, watching the scenery as the large motorhome lumbered along.

"Daddy, are we almost there?" Chelsea asked, her car seat strapped into the couch.

"Yeah, honey, only anther five minutes," Jason said in a loud whisper. He glanced over at Carrie, snoring softly in the passenger seat. Curt was in front of them on the road, Kyle behind with Kate next to him on the bench seat again. She looked asleep in the rear-view mirror.

Route 277 was sparse compared to the gentle hill country terrain Jason lived in. Less trees. More arid. Not desert like West Texas, but getting there. He could see I-10 looming in the distance, and the speed limit was coming down as he neared it. He followed Curt under the I-10 overpass, slowing more as they got into the sleepy little town. The sign for North

Crockett Avenue appeared, and he watched as Curt slowed and took the left turn.

The RV Park was three blocks to the right, off Third Street. Curt made the turn. It was a little tight, so Jason took note and made the turn nice and wide. He saw Kyle in the rear view doing the same thing after he straightened out. Carrie woke up.

"Oh, we there already?" she asked, stretching.

"Yep," he said. "Want to take out Dingo while I go pay?"

"Sure," she said.

"Can I come too, mommy?" Chelsea asked.

"Of course, honey," she said.

They got out of the coach, Dingo prancing around, happy to be outside. Kyle and Kate walked up hand in hand.

"This place actually looks better than I expected," Kyle said.

"The pool isn't open, though," Kate said. "It's dry. Looks pretty trashed."

"No problem," Jason said. "We're just here to sleep and re-group."

"What a garden spot," Curt said, walking up. "I'm so tired. Glad it was only a short drive."

"Seriously," Kyle said. "Maybe we should try to stay awake a little bit longer, though. Get our sleeping back into sync."

"Let's talk about that when we get settled," Curt said. "There *is* something to be said for traveling at night, you know."

"True," Jason said. "We'll chat, maybe have a beer or two. Sound good?"

"Yeah," Curt said. "Let's go settle up and get parked."

They went into the office. There was a short, round old man behind the counter, fly swatter in his hand.

"Dammit," he said, watching the fly buzz by his face. "I'll get you, you son of a bitch."

"Good afternoon," Curt said.

The man took his focus off the fly and looked over, annoyed. "What the hell do you want?"

Curt laughed. "We called a little while ago. You remember, don't you? Three rigs."

"Oh," he said, calming down. The man looked like a troll, with tufts of white hair coming out of his scalp, face, and ears. "Sorry. Damn fly's been messing with me all day."

"No problem," Curt said.

"Good thing you folks called ahead. Phone's been ringing off the hook for the last couple of hours. Everybody's got their panties in a bunch."

"Really?" Kyle asked.

"Yeah," he said. "You look like a cop."

"I do?" Kyle asked. "Is that a problem?"

"Are you?" the old man asked.

"Yeah," Kyle said. "All three of us are."

"Oh, shit," he said. "You aren't gonna cause no trouble are you?"

"You don't like cops?" Jason asked.

"Oh, some of them are okay, like those guys who blasted the pajama boys in Dripping Springs."

Kyle and Jason glanced at each other. Curt walked away laughing while Kate snickered.

"What's so damn funny?" the old man asked.

"Those two *are* the cops from the Dripping Springs attack," Kate said. "Their boss told them to disappear for a few days."

The old man smiled and slapped his knee. "Well I'll be bushwhacked. Welcome. I'm Quincy, but my friends call me Brushy."

"Brushy, huh," Curt said, walking back over, his eyes still dancing with laughter. "These two pencil necks just got lucky in Dripping Springs."

Kyle cracked up. "Yeah, whatever." He turned to Brushy. "You ain't gonna advertise that we're here, are you?"

"Why would I do that?" he asked. "Damn city folks, thinking everybody out here is a fool."

"Calm down, Brushy, it's okay," Kate said. "We're a little paranoid. Been attacked twice, and some of those jerks killed Jason's parents."

"Yeah, saw that on the news," he said. "Real sorry about that."

"The Islamists have gotten the worst part of it so far," Curt said. "Hell, even Kate here blasted some of them, both at the Superstore in Dripping Springs, and last night at our camp site."

"They following you guys?" Brushy asked, eyes darting around. "Better make sure my shotgun is loaded."

"Don't worry, they don't know where we are now," Curt said.

"How do you know that, young fella?"

Curt pulled out his phone and showed it to the old man. "See that? It shows me if we're being tracked. They aren't around here right now. They went east."

"Where'd you get that app?" Brushy asked.

"Took it over from the Islamists," he said. "They were tracking my phone. I turned their app against them."

Brushy laughed hard. "Nice. You'll warn me if they come a calling, right?"

"Oh, yeah, you can count on that," Curt said. "I don't expect them, though. We dumped all the phones they were tracking except this one, and they can't track it anymore."

"Where you goin'?"

"West," Jason said. "To join some others."

"Okay," he said. "You guys look bushed. I'll get your spaces set up."

"Thanks, Brushy," Kate said.

He nodded as he filled out the tags.

"You got a land line around here?" Jason asked.

"Yeah, over there," he said. "Why?"

"Need to call Austin PD later. I can use my cell phone in a pinch, but I'd rather not until we're sure we can't get re-acquired by the Islamists."

"Well, be my guest," Brushy said. "We're having barbecue later, if you guys are interested. Six thirty. You can come for free. Most people are getting charged."

"We might just take you up on that, after we get a nap," Curt said.

"Good, hope to see you," Brushy said. He slid the three tags over to them with maps. "Enjoy. Good to have you here."

"Thanks," Curt said. They turned and walked out the door.

"Get a load of that guy," Kyle said.

"Told you he was a hoot," Curt said. "Let's go."

Carrie was just getting back to the coach. "What are you guys grinning about?"

"That old man in there," Kate said. "Colorful guy. He invited us for barbecue later. Think it's time for a nap now, though."

"Yeah, you got that right. Even Chelsea will take one now. Been a long couple of days."

They got back to their rigs. Curt drove into the park, the other two following. Their spaces were near the center, pull-through spaces with trees shading them. They got set up in a few minutes and met outside.

"So, naps, then some barbecue with Brushy?" Curt asked.

"Brushy?" Carrie asked.

Kate laughed. "That's his nickname."

"Geez," she said. "Fine with me. What time?"

"Six thirty," Jason said. "Gives us about five hours to sleep."

"Good," Carrie said. "I'm done. Hitting the sack. See you all later."

"Be there in just a second, honey," Jason said, watching her lead Chelsea and Dingo inside. Kate turned and went to the trailer, nodding at Kyle on the way.

"That's her hurry-up nod," Curt said to Kyle. "It's starting already. When's the wedding?"

"I could see that happening," Kyle said, looking embarrassed. "She's a keeper."

"She's hot enough to hold a guy's interest," Curt said. "No offence."

"None taken," Kyle said. "Why we still out here?"

"Just had a couple questions for Curt," Jason said.

"Shoot."

"You sure that phone can't be traced?"

"I'm sure," Curt said. "I know how their app worked. It's pretty simple stuff. I'm way ahead of them. What else?"

"Will the alarm wake you if they're coming this way?" Jason asked.

"Sure will," he said. "Don't worry, we'll be fine."

"Okay, that's it for me," Jason said. "You guys got anything?"

"Not me," Kyle said. "Bed awaits."

"Yeah, see that you sleep at least a little," Curt said to Kyle. "I'm good. Always have guns nearby, though, okay?"

"We do," Jason said. "Don't you worry about that."

Curt smiled. "Okay, see you guys a little later."

They retired to their coaches.

Jason woke up to his cellphone alarm at six in the evening. Carrie was still sleeping. He got up and went into the salon. Chelsea was sitting at the dinette table with her coloring books.

"When did you get up, honey?" Jason asked.

"A little while ago," she said.

"You should have woken one of us up before you came out here."

"I wasn't going anywhere. I know I can't go outside."

"Well, next time wake one of us, okay?"

"Okay, daddy," she said. "I'm hungry."

"We're going to go to a barbecue in a little while," Jason said.

"Think they have hot dogs?"

"I don't know honey. We'll see." Jason got his laptop out of the closet and set it up on the dinette table next to Chelsea's coloring books. "Move over a little, sweetie."

"Okay, daddy," Chelsea said.

Dingo growled, waking up on the floor between the front seats.

"Shhh," Jason said, getting up and rushing to the door. He looked out and saw Curt standing by the back of his toy hauler.

"Is it okay, daddy?" Chelsea asked. "There aren't going to be bangs again, are there?"

"No, sweetie, it's just Uncle Curt," he said. "I'm going to go talk to him. Tell mommy if she wakes up, okay? Stay in the coach."

"Okay, daddy," she said.

Jason opened the door as quietly as he could and stepped out. Curt saw him and grinned.

"Get enough sleep?"

"Yeah, Curt. You?"

"Slept like a baby, but I always do in this thing. I'm going to full-time for a while when I decide where to settle."

"We may all be doing that for a while," Jason said. "Hope nobody messes with the house while we're gone."

"You could move out to your dad's spread if you wanted," Curt said. "Love that place."

"Eric and I are gonna have to figure that one out, but I don't see moving out there now. Too far from work."

"Yeah, that's true," he said. "You got a nice spread in Dripping Springs. A little close-in for my taste."

"It's better if you've got kids," Kyle said. "And we're having another."

"I can see that, I guess," he said. "Check out my garage." Curt unlocked the latches on the back of his rig and lowered the ramp. The Barracuda sat inside, gun barrel pointing outward. On the sides and behind it were work benches, cabinets, and tools.

"You took out the furniture," Jason said. "One of my friends has the same model. His has a bed that comes down from the ceiling and couches that fold down on either side near the entrance."

"I ripped all that stuff out," Curt said. "No need for it. C'mon up."

They walked up the ramp. "That your 3-D printer setup?" Jason asked, walking to the workbench against the front wall.

"Yeah," he said. "Amazing what you can do with these things now."

"Ammo reloading equipment. That's good. And a lathe," Jason said, looking at the driver's side wall.

"Comes in handy. I had a small vertical mill, but with the new 3-D printer, I didn't need it anymore. Saved me some weight."

"This is nice," Jason said. "Hell, you even got a fridge and sink out here."

He grinned, walking to it and opening it up. The fridge was chock-full of beer.

"What a shock," Jason said.

"Want one?" Curt asked.

"Sure, why the hell not? We're on vacation."

The two of them chuckled as Kyle walked up.

"Get any sleep, lover boy?" Curt asked as he handed Kyle a beer.

"Yeah, we laid off each other," he said, taking a swig. "Nice setup, man."

"I like it," Curt said. "When the heat dies down, we need to go to my place outside of San Antonio. I've got several more of those auto grenade launchers there."

"What do you have in mind?" Jason asked.

"Well, you got four-wheel drive vehicles. How'd you like to have guns on them?"

Jason laughed. "If things stay crazy, I'd be interested. I'm hoping this will settle down and the government will take control of the problem."

Curt laughed. "I was in a meeting shortly before I got put on leave. They had some estimates that didn't sound too good."

"What?" Kyle asked.

"Four to five hundred thousand enemy fighters already inside Texas, with several hundred thousand more on the way from the south, east, and west."

"Really?" Kyle said. "We heard there was a big problem, but not that big."

"How'd you get in so much trouble with San Antonio PD?" Jason asked. "Why'd you get kicked off the force?"

"I'm still on leave," Curt said. *"Pending an investigation."*

"You punched a superior officer?" Kyle asked. "Really?"

Curt nodded.

"Why'd you do that, anyway?" Jason asked.

"The department was drawing up plans for martial law," Curt said. "Including *temporary* gun confiscation."

"They'll never get away with that," Jason said. "Not even in Austin."

"Austin and San Antonio are two very different cities," Curt said. "Austin has a lot of your garden-variety nuts, and they make a lot of noise. They're a nuisance, but that's about it. Ever hear Chief Ramsey talk about restricting liberty?"

"Hell no," Kyle said.

"San Antonio is run by the open-border crowd now. They're fanatics on protecting the rights of *immigrants,* and they have a complacent police chief who only cares about his damn cushy retirement."

"By immigrants, you're talking about illegals, right?" Jason asked.

"Of course," Curt said. "I got nothing against *legal* immigrants. Anyway, I got into an argument with some brass over this. That's why I threw the punch."

"Do you really believe those numbers?" Kyle asked.

"Oh, yeah, I believe them," he said. "Wish I could say different."

Kate and Carrie walked up with Chelsea. "You guys drinking already?" Carrie asked.

"I'm hungry, daddy," Chelsea said.

"He said six-thirty, right?" Kate asked.

"Yep," Kyle said. "Let's go."

"Yeah," Curt said.

Jason and Kyle got out of the garage, and Curt closed the ramp. The group walked to the main building. Brushy was standing in front of a huge 55-gallon drum barbecue, slathering meat with sauce using a long brush.

"That smells pretty damn good," Curt said as they walked up.

"Hey, how you doing?" Brushy asked, smiling as he turned towards them.

"We got some sleep," Jason said. "That's a good thing."

"Not much of a crowd yet," Carrie said.

"Oh, Brushy, this is my wife Carrie," Jason said. "And my daughter Chelsea."

"Good to meet you," Brushy said. "You're pregnant, aren't you?"

"Yep," Carrie said. "Three months."

"Do you have any hot dogs?" Chelsea asked.

"Sure do," Brushy said. "Just haven't put them on the grill yet. They don't take as long to cook."

"Goody," Chelsea said.

"You folks make yourselves at home. There's ice beer in that washtub over there."

"Thanks," Kyle said.

"Here comes some more folks," Curt said, looking over at them and smiling.

"Welcome, folks," Brushy said. "Have a beer. Over in the washtub."

"Thanks," said a large man with black hair and a beard, wearing biker garb. His woman was next to him, a small and dainty bleach blonde with an edge. He walked to the wash tub and grabbed a beer. His woman got one too.

"Don't drink too much, Gray," she said. "They keep showing up."

"I'm pretty sure we lost them by now," he said, taking a swig of the beer.

"Where you from, friend?" Curt asked.

"Rio Grande Valley," he said. "You?"

"San Antonio. I'm Curt."

"Gray," the man said. "This is Cindy."

"Nice to meet you," she said, trying to smile, her eyes darting around nervously.

"Scared?" Curt asked.

"Don't," Gray said to her.

"Oh, stuff it, Gray," she said. "We've had terrorists chasing us all the way. They keep popping up."

"Islamists, right?" Curt said.

"You a cop?" Gray asked.

"I'm on leave," Curt said. "They been hunting you, huh?"

"Yes," Cindy said. Gray shot her a harsh glance.

Curt smiled. "They were doing the same to us until we found out how they were tracking us."

"Why would they be tracking you?" Gray asked.

"See those guys over there, with the two women and the little girl?"

"Yeah," Gray said. "They with you?"

"Yep," he said. "They were involved in that attack at the Superstore in Dripping Springs."

"Really?" Gray asked. Cindy looked sick to her stomach.

Curt got close enough to whisper. "The Islamists hacked Austin PD's cell phones. Everybody who talked to an infected phone got a virus. It gave control of the phones over to the enemy. They got control of the microphone, camera, GPS, files, everything."

"Oh, shit," Gray said, hand going to his pocket.

"I can tell if you've been hacked. Let's see your phone."

Gray resisted, but Cindy grabbed Gray's phone out of his hand and handed it to Curt.

"Open the screen," Curt said, handing it back.

Gray nodded and punched in his code. Curt took it back and moved his hand over the screen. "Yep," he said. "I can turn this around on them. It'll allow us to see where they are."

"Do it," Cindy said. Gray nodded reluctantly.

Curt moved his fingers on the phone, taking about three minutes to change the tracking program. Then he shut down the phone and counted to thirty.

"What are you doing?" Gray asked.

"Reboot. I reversed their tracking program," Curt said. "Did the same to my phone. Look."

Curt pulled out his phone and showed the program. "The people who've been on my phone aren't there, but if they were, you'd see dots on the map."

"Or your program doesn't work," Gray said.

Curt chuckled, handing Gray's phone back to him. "Log back in."

Gray did that. "Okay, looks normal."

"Punch that icon in the lower middle of the first screen."

His eyes got big as he saw the new icon. He hit it, and an alarm went off.

"Son of a bitch," Curt said. "Hey, Kyle and Jason, we're about to have company."

"What does that mean?"

"Islamists on the way. See those dots there on the map display? We got about ten minutes. You guys have guns?"

"Yeah," Gray said. "I'll go get the others."

Kyle and Jason ran over. "What?"

"This is Gray," Curt said. "He was being tracked. I reversed his app. They're coming."

"Oh, shit," Jason said, rushing back over to the women.

"Brushy," Curt said. "We're about to have some Islamic guests."

"Ah, crap," he said. "Did they follow you here?"

"No, they followed Gray here. He had a hacked cellphone."

"Tarnation," Brushy said. "My damn meat's gonna burn."

"Pull it off the grill and get your gun," Curt said. "You can cook it the rest of the way after we've iced these creeps."

Brushy laughed. "I'm starting to like you, boy."

"We got about ten minutes," Curt said. "There a PA system here? Might want to warn the other residents."

"Yeah," he said.

"Get your guns," Curt said to Gray. "Hope your people know how to fight."

"They do," he said. "I'm obliged to you."

"Don't mention it," Curt said. He trotted to catch up with Kyle, Jason, and the women, getting to their campsites in less than a minute.

Brushy's crusty old voice came over the loudspeakers. "Islamist Terrorists are on the way to the park. Get ready. If you have guns, now's the time to get them out."

"Girls, grab the Thompsons," Jason said. "Kyle and I got the BARs."

"Mommy, I'm scared," Chelsea said.

"Get in the bedroom and lay on the floor," Carrie said.

"No," Curt said, running over. "Put her in the back of my rig. I've got Kevlar in the walls. I'm pulling the Barracuda out now."

He rushed to his toy hauler, opened the back gate, and drove the off-roader, out.

"You might want to stay in there with her," Curt said.

"Yeah, I think you're right," Carrie said. "One of you want to take this Thompson? I'll take the mini-14 and my pistol in there."

"Yeah, I'll take it in the Barracuda with me. It loaded?"

"Yeah," Carrie said.

Jason rushed over with his BAR. Curt looked at it and laughed. "Lord have mercy."

"Good, I was gonna suggest you take her into the garage," Jason said. "Curt said it has Kevlar in the walls."

"Yeah," she said. "The side door too?"

"Yep, except the window, of course," Curt said, "but not the salon, and if somebody hits you with something big, get the hell out fast. It'll probably blow."

"Got it," Carrie said. Curt and Jason pushed the ramp closed.

"This bullet proof?" Jason asked.

"Against an AK-47? Yeah," Curt said. "Against your BAR, probably not for long." He chuckled, then pulled out his cellphone and made a call.

"Who you calling?"

"Gray, that guy with the hacked phone. I want to pick up what he has." He put the phone to his ear.

"Who's this?" Gray asked.

"Curt. I needed to call to pick up your virus."

"Why would you want to do that?" Gray asked.

"So I can see where the bad guys are coming in. You should use it for that too. You guys well-armed?"

"We got some captured AK-47s and a bunch of hunting rifles. What do you guys have?"

Curt laughed. "A couple BARs, a couple Thompsons, and other assorted toys."

"Holy shit, where'd you get BARs and Thompsons?"

"Long story. We'll get acquainted at the barbecue." He paused, looking at the phone screen. "Crap, they're half a block away, coming right down Crockett Street. I'm gonna drive the Barracuda up to the front gate and give them the welcome they deserve."

"What's a Barra...never mind. I hear them coming. Gonna go get my men out there."

Curt stuffed his phone back in his pocket. "They're here," he shouted, driving the Barracuda up to the front of the park.

"You gotta to be kidding me," Brushy said when he saw the off-roader with its big gun. Curt shot him a grin and nodded, then pulled up to the street, just as the first truck was getting there. It was a large troop transport truck. He aimed the Mark 19. The driver and passenger in the cab saw the big barrel pointed at them, eyes getting big as the grenade flew at them. It went through the windshield and blew up, splattering them to bits.

Men jumped out of the back of the truck, only to be hit by fire from Kyle and Jason's BARs and Kate's Thompson machinegun.

"There's two more trucks coming!" Brushy shouted, just as Gray and his people showed up.

Curt drove around the ruined truck and shot the second one, lifting it into the air. Gray's men ran over and opened fire on the men trying to flee from the burning wreckage.

"Hey, Curt, the other one's turning around!" Kyle shouted while reloading his BAR.

"I see them," Curt shouted, driving around the second truck. He sped up, shooting a grenade at the back. It flew inside and blew up, killing the men in the back, but the truck kept rolling. "Dammit." He floored the Barracuda, but he was close to full speed already, and the truck was extending its lead fast. Curt fired off another grenade, and it went through to the wall between the cab and the back of the truck, blowing up, sending the truck flying into a ditch. He rolled up behind it. Two men were running away. Curt picked up the Thompson, pulled back the bolt, and opened fire, hitting both of the men.

Kyle and Kate arrived, holding their weapons. "Get them all?"

"Yeah, I think so," Curt said. "Let's grab their guns and ammo."

"Good idea," Kyle said.

"I'll grab their phones too," Kate said.

Back at camp, Gray's men were sifting through the wreckage, picking up anything that looked valuable. Jason walked up. Gray looked at his weapon.

"Where the hell did you get that BAR?"

"My father had a collection," he said. "I'm Jason. You must be Gray."

"Yeah," he said. "Curt is quite a character. Glad we ran into you guys." Brushy came out of the office, double barrel shotgun in his hand.

"Hey Brushy, you gonna call the cops?" Jason.

"Maybe after we eat," Brushy said. "I'd better get that meat back on the grill." He went to the barbecue, picking up a big tray covered with foil, using his tongs to put the meat back on the grill.

"He's kidding, right?" Cindy asked.

"I doubt it," Jason said. He saw Kyle and Kate walking back over.

"Gray, this is my partner Kyle and his girlfriend Kate," Jason said.

"Good to meet you folks," Gray said.

"Likewise," Kyle said. "You guys did a good job on that second truck."

"Yeah, after Curt split it wide open," Gray said. "What the hell is that thing he has mounted on top?"

"Mark 19 Automatic Grenade Launcher," Kyle said. "You got his app, right? Better check it and make sure no more *guests* are on the way."

"Good idea," Gray said. He pulled out his phone and looked. "Don't see anybody."

"Good," Jason said. "I'm gonna go get Carrie and Chelsea."

"Keep your guns on you," Brushy said. Jason nodded as he was walking away.

"None of the other residents came out," Kyle said.

"Most of them are older folks fleeing the trouble," Brushy said. "I suspect some of them will be leaving in a few minutes."

Curt drove back into the park, grinning ear to ear. "Well that was fun."

Brushy turned towards him from the grill, the meat sizzling again. "Nice toy you got there."

"Thanks," he said. "Almost lost that last truck. This thing is fast for the dirt, but on the street just about anything can outrun it."

Gray and his men gathered around. They were a collection of old bikers. Most of them already had beers in their hands.

"Where'd you get that grenade launcher?" Gray asked.

"Trade secret," he said. "I made the gimbal and sight assembly with my 3-D printer and some surplus electronics."

"Do tell," Gray said. "Love to mount something like that on my Harley."

Curt laughed. "Hell, that would have been good today. I doubt that truck can outrun a Harley."

Jason returned with Carrie and Chelsea.

"How'd it go in there?" Kate asked Carrie.

"It was scary not being able to see what was going on outside," she said. "The Kevlar does a good job of sound isolation. We could hear the gunfire, but it was really muffled."

"Really?" Curt asked. "I'll have to remember that."

"You gonna put the Barracuda away?" Kyle asked.

"No, I think I'll leave her out for now. The phone app has a pretty short range. There may be more *company* before the night is over."

"You said the phone app is like a virus," Gray said. "I've talked to all my men with this phone. Should we do something about that?"

"Yeah," Curt said. "Bring them to me. I'll reverse the apps on all of them."

"Maybe we shouldn't have dumped our phones," Jason said.

"You didn't have a choice," Curt said. "You didn't know how to reverse them."

"Where you guys headed?" Gray asked.

"West," Jason said. "You?"

"Hell, I don't know," Gray said. "We've just been running."

"How'd you get on these guy's radar?"

"Caught a bunch of them coming over the Rio Grande. We fought them. Killed a bunch, but they captured some of our people. Beheaded them."

"And got their cellphones," Curt said. "Some of your men tried to call them."

"Yep," Gray said.

"There goes the first one," Brushy said, waving as a big motor home with an old couple behind the windshield pulled out. It stopped and the driver opened the side window.

"Sorry, Brushy, we can't stick around. We're too old for this sort of thing."

"Understand, Ken," Brushy said. "Take care."

"You too," he said.

The meat was ready after another ten minutes. The group sat down to eat and talk. After dinner Gray's people lined up in front of Curt, and he took care of their phones. When he was done, he walked over to where Kyle, Jason, and Kate were sitting. It was dark, chill coming in the air.

"Carrie hit the sack already?" he asked.

"Yeah, she's beat, and she took Chelsea to bed," Jason said. "Hope the stress doesn't hurt the baby. I'm worried about her."

"I wouldn't worry about it too much," Kate said. "Women were built to cope with this kind of thing, remember."

"Hope you're right," Jason said. "You got all the phones fixed, Curt?"

"Yeah," he said. "Yanked batteries out of all the enemy phones too, except the iPhones."

"What did you do with those?"

"I'm about to throw them on the fire," he said, nodding to the campfire. "*Find my friends* will work on those. Difficult to shut that off since you can't take the batteries out."

"You think Gray and his folks are gonna want to tag along with us?" Kyle asked.

"Wouldn't surprise me," Curt said. "They're good people. I'd be game. They got a couple of un-attached females, too."

"Saw that," Kate said. "You meet them?"

"Yeah," Curt said. "One of them is interesting."

"We gonna build ourselves a militia?" Jason asked, grinning.

Curt laughed. "Why do you think that?"

"We're gonna meet up with Kelly's people in Fort Stockton, right?" Kyle asked. "I was thinking the same thing."

"True," Curt said. "Could end up working out that way. We could do a lot worse, by the way."

"You sure we should head straight west?" Jason asked. "Maybe we ought to go get the rest of those Mark 19s you have stashed in San Antonio."

"Been thinking about that, but it's really far out of the way." Curt said. "Let's talk tomorrow. We should hit the sack now."

"Sounds good," Jason said. "I'll see you in the morning."

Kate and Kyle stood, glancing over at the front of the office. "Brushy is conked out in that lounge by the door," Kyle said. "Maybe we ought to wake him and get him to bed."

"I'll do it," Curt said. "Got to go over there and dump these iPhones in the fire anyway."

"Okay, see you in the morning,"

{ 12 }

Redneck Contact

Kelly snuck out of bed and got his laptop out as Brenda snored softly. He set it up on the dinette and plugged it in, then got the coffee pot loaded and put it on the front burner of his stove. He glanced out the kitchen window. The sun was coming up.

The laptop got through its boot-up. Kelly grabbed the scrap of paper with Wi-Fi instructions on it and punched in the password. The laptop connected right away. He navigated to his e-mail. Three messages were waiting. One from Nate, one from Jasper, and one from Curt. He smiled and opened the message from Nate.

"You up already?" Brenda asked, walking out of the bedroom, pulling a robe on.

"Yeah, thought I'd see if Nate sent me a message."

"They can get e-mail to you without it being seen?" she asked.

"Far as I know," Kelly said. He watched her slide into the dinette bench across the table from him.

"Get anything?"

"Yeah, messages from Nate, Jasper, and Curt."

"Nothing from Chris?" she asked.

"No," Kelly said. "I'm a little surprised, actually."

"Hope he's okay."

"Might not be Wi-Fi at his sister's place," Kelly said as he opened Nate's e-mail.

Brenda laughed. "Yeah, Chris's sister is technology-challenged."

"Nate got further than we did," Kelly said, reading the message.

"Where's he at?"

"Harper," Kelly said. "Or rather he was in Harper. They left before the sun came up."

Brenda looked at her phone, pulling up the map app. "Hell, that was only forty minutes from here."

"No matter, we'll meet them in Fort Stockton," Kelly said.

"That coffee is smelling good," Brenda said. "Haven't had percolated coffee in a long time. How come you don't have a Keurig?"

"I used to camp in the boondocks a lot," Kelly said. "Electric coffee makers only work where you can plug in, unless you have a generator."

"Oh," she said. "What time are we leaving?"

"Sooner the better," Kelly said. "I'm gonna look at these other messages."

"Okay, I'll get dressed. Want bacon and eggs for breakfast?"

"Sure," Kelly said. He laughed.

"What?"

"Curt," Kelly said. "Look at this picture he sent me."

Brenda looked over his shoulder. "What the hell is that?"

"One heavily armed off-roader," Kelly said. "Typical Curt. He's with those two Austin cops who were at the Superstore attack."

"Really? Where are they now?"

"Sonora," Kelly said. "They're going the same place we are."

"Good," Brenda said. "The more the merrier." She went into the bedroom and dropped the robe. Kelly glimpsed her naked back.

"Nice," he said.

She sighed. "If you want me, get in here now," she said, "before I get dressed."

"Don't have to ask me twice," Kelly said, getting up and rushing into the bedroom, yanking off his robe on the way. They fell onto the bed in a naked embrace, becoming more and more familiar with each other now. What worked, what they liked, their passion fusing them together. They finished, breathing hard, damp with sweat.

"I hope this lasts," Brenda said, lying next to him, eyes on the ceiling.

"Are you afraid it won't?"

"I'm afraid I'll push you away," Brenda said. "I'll try not to."

"How would you push me away?"

"I can be a white-hot bitch," she said, looking at him. "You might tire of that."

"We get along well so far," Kelly said.

"Oh, it always works for a while," she said. "It's usually my fault when it comes crashing down. It was with Chris."

"Stop it," Kelly said. "Do you love me?"

She looked at him, eyes tearing. "It's a little early for that, isn't it?"

"Answer the question," he said.

"I don't want to yet," she said.

"Suit yourself," he said, getting up. "I think I can make you happy. I know you can make me happy."

"Well I hope so," she said, "and that's the truth."

"Gonna go check that last email," Kelly said. He pulled on his pants and a shirt and went back to the dinette.

"Who's it from again?"

"Jasper," Kelly said, sitting in front of the screen. He clicked it open and read. "Jasper and Earl are with Chris and his sister now."

"Thank God," she said, coming out of the bedroom with her clothes on. "Where are they?"

"Way north of us," Kelly said. "Brownwood."

"That figures," Brenda said. "His sister lives in Comanche. They're coming from there."

"What's she like?"

"Quite a bit older than Chris, and ornery as all get out," she said. "You'll like her. We ought to fix her up with Junior. They'd be two peas in a pod." She poured coffee for both of them, then looked back at Kelly. "Did you hear what I said? You look really nervous."

"We got a problem," he said, looking at her.

She set the coffee next to Kelly and sat across from him again. "What's wrong?"

"Simon Orr is with them."

"Oh, dammit," she said. "That's not good."

"No, it's not," Kelly said. "That guy is bad news."

"What should we do? Warn them?"

Robert Boren

"No," Kelly said. "Not yet. Let's wait until we're all together in Fort Stockton."

"Why?"

"Because I don't want that guy to stick a shiv in our friends before we can protect them," Kelly said.

"You think he's that dangerous?" Brenda asked, eyes getting wide.

"I got a really bad vibe from that guy," Kelly said. "Hopefully it's just me, but I don't think so."

There was a knock at the door. Brenda turned towards it, eyes filled with terror.

"Don't worry, that's probably Junior," Kelly said, getting up. He looked out the window. "Yep, he smelled the coffee."

"Good morning, Junior," Kelly said as he opened the door.

"Morning," he said, "and morning to you too, sugar plum."

Brenda smiled. "Sleep well?"

"Yeah," he said. "I love my new coach."

"We can kinda tell," Kelly said, laughing. "Got e-mails from Nate, Curt, and Jasper."

"Good," Junior said. "How about some of that coffee?"

"Help yourself," Kelly said.

He poured himself a cup and then leaned against the counter facing the dinette. Kelly was shutting down his laptop.

"Where are they?" Junior asked.

"Nate's group left Harper early this morning. They're ahead of us."

"What did Curt have to say? Didn't expect to hear from him already."

"He's with those two Austin cops who were at the Superstore attack," Kelly said. "They're ahead of us too. They were in Sonora last night. Probably on the road by now. They'll get to Fort Stockton first."

"How about Jasper?"

"He's with Chris and his sister," Kelly said. "Oh, and Earl's with them."

"Good. Never met Chris's sister."

"You'll like her," Brenda quipped as she got up. "I'll fix breakfast."

"Excellent," Junior said. He sat in the dinette across from Kelly.

{ 13 }

Federal Pressure

K ip Hendrix walked into his office suite. He was earlier than normal. Maria had just arrived.

"Good morning, sir," she said, smiling. He eyed her and smiled.

"Good morning, Maria. Have a nice evening?"

"I did," she said. "My sister came over for a visit. It was nice to have some company."

"You still live alone?" he asked, watching as she puttered with the coffee machine.

"No," she said. "I have my cats with me." She giggled.

"You sound happier than normal," Hendrix said.

"I was worried about my sister," Maria said. "She was living near Zapata."

"Oh," Hendrix said. "Getting dangerous down there."

"Yes," Maria said. "I talked her into moving in with our mother for a while."

"In Austin?"

"Yes," Maria said. She got behind her desk, then backed up and picked something off the floor, not realizing that she was showing too much cleavage until she saw Kip's stare. She sat upright quickly and put her hand to her chest.

"Well, I'm glad she's safe," Hendrix said. He hurried into his office.

"Me too," she said from behind her desk. "I'll bring you coffee in a moment, unless you'd rather have tea."

"Coffee would be good," he said. "I've got to wake up. Had a bad night."

"Oh, I'm sorry," she said. "Something wrong?" She made the cup of coffee and carried it in, being careful not to bend down again when she set it on his desk.

"Oh, I'm just lonely, and worried about all this violence," he said, making eye contact for a second, then looking away.

"Well, hopefully the coffee will help." She walked out to her desk.

Hendrix picked up the newspaper and read as he sipped coffee. Attacks in all the major cities yesterday. Falcon Lake partially overrun by foreign fighters. Protests scheduled for today in Austin about the border closure. Hostage crisis continuing in San Antonio.

The phone rang.

"Sir, it's the US Attorney General's office, line one."

"Thank you, Maria," Hendrix said, heart beating faster. He picked it up.

"Franklin, how are you?"

"Hi, Kip," he said in a Boston accent. "Got a few minutes?"

"I've always got time for the Assistant Attorney General of the United States," Hendrix said, sweat breaking out on his forehead.

"We've been hearing some disturbing rumors," Franklin said. "You know what I'm talking about?"

"Governor Nelson?"

"Yes," Franklin said.

"I've heard the rumors," Hendrix said. "I don't believe most of them."

"Which do you believe?"

"I believe that the border shutdown will be longer term than we've been told."

Franklin chuckled. "Come on, now, everybody knows that."

"I believe that state military is being used on Falcon Lake and the Rio Grande."

{ 169 }

"Again, that is common knowledge. You aren't giving me much. I'm disappointed."

"What do you want me to say? I'm telling you what I believe. I know there're rumors that Nelson is going to declare Texas a sovereign republic, but I doubt that will really happen." Sweat dripped off of Hendrix's forehead, onto his newspaper.

"You're being too cagey," Franklin said. "We can't contact any of the Federal military bases in Texas now. Not a one. The funny thing is that US Air Force assets stationed in Texas are helping the Texas Air National Guard with attacks in Mexico."

"I hadn't heard that," Hendrix said, heart beating quicker.

"Bullshit," Franklin said.

"C'mon, Franklin, what do you want from me?"

"Information. Confirmation. Somebody inside."

"I'm always been willing to share my opinion," Hendrix said.

"So *it is* true, then," Franklin said. "Nelson *is* taking Texas out of the union. You're being cagey because you don't want to be considered a traitor to Texas after the announcement. Treason against the state could land you in prison or worse."

"Don't be ridiculous," Hendrix said.

"Okay, play it that way if you want to," Franklin said. "I'll call upon you after the announcement. You'll be our eyes and ears inside Texas."

"You can't make me do that," Hendrix said, face flushing.

Franklin chuckled. "Oh yes we can. Don't forget about those little problems we helped you push under the rug. How many chiquitas has it been now? Pretty nasty what you did. Pretty expensive to US and Texas taxpayers, too. You could end up with free room and board for quite a while. Hell, Federal and Texas agencies might be fighting over your sorry ass."

"That'll come back on you, too," Hendrix said.

Franklin laughed. "Yeah, but then I'll be just another foreign bureaucrat. The Attorney General's office would protect themselves. Vigorously."

"You'd still get splattered enough to end your career," Hendrix said.

"Well, if it comes to that, we'll see," he said. "You are *excused* for now. We'll be in touch." The call ended. Hendrix stood up, loosening his tie, gasping for air, heart hammering in his chest. He felt himself going numb and crumpled to the floor.

"Sir, what's wrong?" Maria asked, rushing to him, getting down on her knees and checking him for a pulse. He was still alive. "Sir!" she said, shaking him. He woke up to her face above his, her breasts resting on his shoulder. He touched her cheek, and then pulled her face down, kissing her. She stiffened and got up quickly. "Mr. Hendrix, stop that! It's very unprofessional."

"Sorry," he said. "Please forgive me."

She stood above him, looking down as his eyes pleaded. "You can't do that with me. It's not right."

Hendrix got to his feet. "I'm sorry. It's all this stress, and I'm so lonely. I didn't mean anything."

She looked him up and down. "You won't do it again?"

"Not if you don't want it," he said, looking down, shame on his face. Maria watched him as he began to cry.

"Sir," she said softly. "Pull yourself together. You've got meetings coming up shortly."

"I'm so sorry," he said. "Will you forgive me?"

She looked at him for more than a minute, thinking. Then she sighed. "All right, sir, as long as it doesn't happen again. And quit looking at my chest. It makes me uncomfortable."

"I'm sorry," he said. "It's just that you're so beautiful."

"You need to find a girlfriend," she said.

"I'd like it to be you," he said.

She shook her head. "You're old enough to be my father. Find somebody your own age. There's plenty of attractive women who would love to be with a powerful man like you. You're still handsome enough, and you *can* be charming."

"So there's no chance?"

"No, sir, there's no chance," she said. "Do I have to resign?"

"No, no, please don't do that," he said. "I'll behave. I promise."

She sat down on a chair in front of his desk. "What got you so upset? I've never seen you like this."

"Can you keep a secret?"

"Yes, sir, but don't tell me if you shouldn't."

"As long as you don't tell, it's fine. It's not classified or anything like that. It would make me feel better to talk to somebody about it. Somebody I can trust."

Maria's face went from worry and revulsion to intense interest.

Hendrix studied her face. *This is my way in.* "You promise not to say anything? It'll stay between us?"

"Yes," she said, eyes dilated.

"Governor Nelson is going to declare Texas a sovereign republic. We're breaking away from the United States."

Maria's pulse quickened, her eyes getting wider. "Really? Why?"

"Because of the invasion," Hendrix said. "The Governor believes that the Federal Government has been corrupted by the enemy and is working against the states and the people."

"Is he correct?" Maria asked.

"Partially," Hendrix said. "It's a very complex issue. I can't say too much here. If you want to know more, we should go someplace else."

"Sir," she said.

"No, no, I didn't mean that," Hendrix said.

"Why can't you talk about it here?" she asked.

"The walls might have ears."

"Why did the US Attorney General's office call you?" Maria asked. "Do they know about this?"

"They heard rumors, and wanted me to confirm them," he said.

"They threatened you, didn't they?"

"Yes," he said. "They want me to spy on Texas for the Federal Government."

"Oh," Maria said. "Now I get it."

"There's a lot more going on, but that's all I'll talk about here," he said. "If you want to hear more, it must be someplace else. Maybe over lunch or dinner or something. *Talk only.*"

She sat back in her chair, thinking. "I'm not sure if I can trust you, Mr. Hendrix. I won't be your office plaything."

"That's not what I wanted anyway," Hendrix said.

"You stare at my breasts and my butt all the time," she said. "We women know what that means, you know."

Hendrix smiled at her. "Of course I want you, but I didn't want you for some fling that would be over after a one-night stand. I wanted a relationship with you. I'm lonely. Don't you understand that?"

"Our ages are too far apart," she said. "I'm sorry."

"I understand," he said, "but anyway, if you want to discuss this more, I'm willing, just not here. At least it would help with the loneliness, even if we can't be intimate. Having somebody to confide in makes a big difference."

"I'll think about it," she said, standing up. Hendrix made sure he only looked at her eyes, and she noticed. "Your first appointment is in half an hour. You sure you're all right? You passed out."

Hendrix laughed. "I fainted, but only for a few seconds. I'll be okay. I don't like to be threatened, but it helped a lot talking to you about it. Don't worry, I'm ready for my day."

"Okay, sir," she said as she left. Hendrix smiled as he went back to the newspaper. *I have her now.*

{ 14 }

Carthage

The wooded scenery of east Texas rolled by.

"How long do we stay on State Route 2517?" Kim asked.

"A little while longer," Eric said. "Antioch road is coming up, as I remember. We take that north to Carthage."

"We can make it there before dark?"

"It's gonna be close," he said. "There was a nice RV Park there, on Route 79, heading out of Carthage. That's the road we want to be on. We should see if we can get in there."

"Wish we had our phones," Kim said.

"Yeah, it's a real pain. I resisted smart phones for quite a while. Now I have a hard time getting by without them."

"You think Dirk and his guys are gonna be okay out there?" Kim asked.

"I don't know. Deadwood is pretty small. If I was them I'd pack up and split."

"You think there's going to be more Islamists coming in from that direction?"

"I think it's possible, because the border is easy to sneak across there. Hell, we did it."

Paco trotted up to the front, looking up at Kim. "Okay, Paco, come on," she said, patting her lap.

"Hey, buddy," Eric said.

"He doesn't get spooked with the gunfire," Kim said.

"Yeah, noticed that. I'm surprised. It's not like he's a hunting dog."

Kim laughed. "He'd be great at hunting field mice."

"Be nice," Eric said. "He's a real killer. Look at that face."

"Right," Kim said. "I love him. You know that."

"He *does* have a way of winning you over. I wasn't wanting a dog when I got him."

"How did you get him?"

"Friend of mine," Eric said. "He got evicted, and couldn't afford a place that allowed pets. I took him *temporarily*."

Kim laughed. "Yeah, looks real temporary."

"The friend went back to California. I haven't heard from him for over two years."

"You wouldn't give him up now anyway, would you?"

"No way," Eric said. "He's family."

"Softy."

"Hey, you found me out," Eric said.

They rode along silently for a while, Kim dozing off a couple of times, then waking up and watching Eric, her affection for him almost overpowering.

Eric caught her staring at him and smiled. "Look, there's our road already." Kim looked at him, embarrassed, as he made the right turn.

"How big is this city?" she asked.

"Lots bigger than Deadwood," Eric said.

"Good, maybe I can get some more clothes while we're there."

"Shouldn't be a problem," Eric said, "but let's get set up at the RV Park first, before the office closes on us. Be dark in less than an hour."

"Okay," she said. "The road changed names. Now it's Forsythe Road."

"Yep," he said. "Forgot about that."

"We're getting into town now," she said. "Lots of industrial here."

"Lots of residential on our left," Eric said.

"Look at that big factory there," she said, pointing out the driver's side window. "Wonder what they do there?"

"Don't know. Highway 79 is right up ahead."

"There's a sign for the Country Music Hall of Fame," Kim said. "Ever been there?"

"Nah," Eric said. "Left turn ahead. This stretch gets tricky. Highway 79 jogs. Maybe it's better now that the Hall of Fame is here. It's on the road we need to take."

"Yeah, at least there's plenty of signs to lead you to that road," Kim said.

He made the left turn, onto Sabine Road. "This is coming back to me fast. Hasn't changed much in the last ten years."

"This is a nice town." Kim said.

"A little too sleepy for me," Eric said. "The quiet can be good, though, I guess. Maybe this is a good place to ride out the troubled times."

"There's a sign up there, for the Hall of Fame and Route 79. Take a right on Sycamore."

"Yeah, and then a left on Panola Street," Eric said. He turned right and then left.

"There's the Hall of Fame," Kim said. "Big brick building. Looks pretty nice."

"Yeah," he said as they drove past it.

"How much further to the park?"

"Fifteen minutes," Eric said. "Maybe less. We go under the freeway overpass, and through the country about five miles.

"I see the freeway bridge up ahead," Kim said. "Where does that go?"

"Around the city," Eric said.

"Look, there's an H-E-B, and some other shops."

"Yeah, we should come back here in the Bronco. You can get clothes, and we can get some groceries. We're low on a few things."

They rode past that, into pasture land with occasional stands of trees and structures.

"Big petro-plant," Kim said, pointing to the left.

"I remember that. We're almost to the RV Park. It's on the left, a mile down."

"I see the sign," She pointed ahead. "See it?"

"Yep, see it," he said. He made the turn into the staging area and parked.

"Not many amenities," Kim said.

"They have hook-ups. That's all we need for an overnighter."

"Want me to take Paco out while you get us a spot?"

"Sure," he said. Both of them got out. Eric walked into the office as Kim took Paco around.

"Hi," Eric said as he walked to the counter. A middle aged woman leaned on it, smiling. She had dishwater blonde hair in a permanent, giving her a 1960s look, with an attractive figure for her age.

"Hi yourself," she said. "I'm Charlene. Need a space?"

"Eric," he said. "Yes, we need a spot for a Class C towing a Bronco. I've got a small dog."

"No problem," she said. "You're lucky. We were full up until last night."

"Really? Why'd everybody leave?"

"Rumors that terrorists were on their way here," she said. "Wish I could afford to clear out."

"That doesn't sound good," he said. "You actually see any terrorists, or we just talking rumors?"

"Rumors," she said. "Maybe people are just upset because of what happened in the big cities yesterday."

"Maybe," Eric said, reaching for his wallet. "How much?"

"Just one night? Thirty."

"You got Wi-Fi?"

Charlene chuckled. "Yeah, we got it, but it's slower than molasses in winter time. Good enough for e-mail, but that's about it. It's free, though."

"That'll work for me," Eric said.

She slipped the tag to him with a map. "Wi-Fi password is on there. Don't need codes for the restrooms or showers."

"Good, thanks," he said. "Have a nice evening."

"You too," she said.

Eric walked to the rig, getting there as Kim brought Paco back.

"All set?" she asked.

"All set. How'd Paco do?"

"Great," she said.

They got into the motor home and Eric drove to the spot.

"Well, it *is* pretty," Kim said. "Look at the trash cans. They're almost full, but it doesn't look like this place gets much business."

"The park was full yesterday, but people flew the coop last night," Eric said. "The lady in the office said there's been rumors of terrorists coming this way."

"Crap," she said. "We gonna be safe here?"

"I hope so, but we stay armed all the time," Eric said. "Let's get set up quick, and then make that store run."

"Okay," Kim said.

Eric got the hook-ups done in about five minutes, and then unhitched the Bronco, pulling it up next to the side door of the motor home.

"You want me to feed Paco?" she asked out the door.

"Yeah, go for it," Eric said. "I'll be there in a minute."

Eric got out and walked around the space, looking at the curtain of woods that bounded three sides of the park. *Good place for an ambush.* He went into the coach just as Kim was putting the food dish in front of Paco.

"Everything okay?" she asked.

"Yeah, I'm just nervous," he said. "Ready to go?"

"In a minute. I want to run a brush through my hair. Maybe we can get a bite to eat while we're there. There was a pizza joint in that shopping center."

"I'm good with that," Eric said.

They locked the coach and took off in the Bronco as darkness approached.

"Where we going tomorrow?" Kim asked.

"I think we're about five hours from Austin," Eric said. "Maybe we ought to just go for it."

"Which road?" she asked.

"It's 79 the whole way," Eric said.

"Any good stops that are part way there?" she asked. "In case you don't want to drive that far in one day?"

"Marquez," Eric said. "That's about half way. Pretty small town. Maybe we ought to listen to the radio tonight. I don't know where the dangerous places are, but you can bet there are some, with everything going on."

"There's the shopping center."

"Good," Eric said. "Look, there's a Sears outlet over there. I think they have cell phones."

"Really?" Kim asked. "I'd love to get phones. Think we can keep them from getting hacked again?"

"If we're careful," Eric said. "Let's get clothes, then phones, then go to H-E-B, then get pizza on the way out. Get one big enough for leftovers. Cold pizza is good food for the road."

"Sounds good, honey," she said, watching him again as he parked the Bronco. He caught her watching.

"What?" he asked.

"I'm so happy," she said.

"Even with all of this?"

"I'd rather be in this world with you than anywhere else without you," she said.

He smiled at her. "C'mon, let's go."

They got out of the Bronco and went clothes shopping. Eric's eyes darted around while Kim was trying things on, but he tried to hide his nervousness while she was with him. Something wasn't right. Everybody was scared. He could smell it.

"I think these will hold me," Kim said, coming out of the changing room with a bundle of clothes. "Not that much I like here."

"Okay," Eric said. They paid, and then walked over to the Sears outlet. It was closed.

"Dammit," Kim said, "Guess we have to go without phones for a little longer."

"Surprised they're closed and the clothing place is open," Eric said, "Strange." His eyes continued to dart around as they walked to the H-E-B.

"You're really nervous," she said, watching his face.

"I'm okay, sweetie," he said, "Just tired."

"Talk to me," she said. "Don't shut me out. I can take it."

Eric sighed. "Okay. Everybody here is scared. Can't you feel it?"

"No, but it does bother me that the place is so deserted," she said. "You think we're okay?"

"Yeah, but I'm glad we're almost done." They walked into the grocery store and froze, looking at half-empty shelves and harried checkers.

"Now I'm scared," Kim said. "Looks like a hurricane is coming. Seen that more than once in Florida. And now it's deserted."

"I know," Eric said. "Let's get what we need and get the hell out of here."

She nodded, and they grabbed a cart and raced through the store. The canned goods were almost gone, but there was still perishable and frozen food left. They took what they had to the checkout. The checker was relieved to see somebody. She was a heavy-set brunette, about thirty years old.

"Sorry we're so short on stuff," she said. "Got a truck coming in, but not till tomorrow afternoon."

"People are hoarding, aren't they?" Kim asked.

"Yeah," she said as she moved items over the reader. "I stocked up, but I don't know why. All we got is rumors at this point. The problems have been way east and south, except for what happened in Dallas."

"Are people leaving town?" Eric asked.

"Some, but most are just hunkering down." She finished scanning the items and totaled them. Eric paid, and they pushed the cart out to the Bronco.

"Less cars here than there were," Kim said.

"You're right," Eric said. "Could just be because it's getting later."

"Maybe," she said. "We still getting pizza?"

"I'm game, but if you'd rather get back I'm fine with it."

She thought about it for a moment. "It's okay, let's get the pizza."

"All right," Eric said. They got into the Bronco and drove it around to the front of the shopping center. The pizza joint was dark.

"It's closed," Kim said. "Let's get out of here."

"Yeah," Eric said, getting on Route 79 and racing all the way home, the dark road deserted. Both of them were relieved when they pulled next to their motor home.

"You gonna hitch the Bronco back up?" Kim asked.

"I want to think about it a little," Eric said, getting out. He went to the tailgate and opened it, grabbing several bags. Kim took a few more, and they went inside with them.

"Couple more out there," Kim said.

"I'll get them and lock up."

"Okay." She put things away as Paco watched her.

Eric came back in. "I'm not going to hitch it back up, just in case we have to leave in a hurry. We'll never get away in this motor home."

"Makes sense," Kim said. "Let's have the frozen mac 'n cheese for dinner, okay? We can microwave it."

"Fine by me," he said.

"You want a beer?"

"No, I'd rather stay straight tonight. You go ahead if it'll calm you down, though."

"I'll pass. Why don't you try the radio?"

"I'll do that," Eric said.

"Wonder if the Wi-Fi is any good?"

"Charlene said it sucked, but it's good enough for e-mail," Eric said. "I'll try it. Need to check my e-mail. Might be something from Jason."

"Turn on the radio first, okay?" Kim asked as she checked dinner. "Food's almost done."

"Good." Eric went to the driver's seat and turned on the dash radio. He hit seek on the AM band, skipping over the scratchy country-western stations and religious sermons. He found a network affiliate and turned it up. "Almost to the top of the hour. Should be something."

"Thanks, honey," she said, walking to meet him as he left the driver's seat. She put her arms around his waist and pulled him close, kissing him passionately. He moaned and leaned into her. She broke the kiss and looked into his eyes. "I'm scared."

"It'll be okay," he said. "We're off the beaten path here. We'll be fine overnight."

"Unless we aren't," she said. "I'll want you tonight."

"Good," he said.

The microwave dinged. Kim glanced at it. "Should be ready. I'll dish it up."

"Thanks," he said. "Nothing on the news we didn't already know about."

"Turn it off, then. We can always check out the web on your laptop later."

They ate their meal quietly. Paco came over, whining.

"He wants to go out," Kim said.

"I know," Eric said. "Want to go?"

"Yeah," she said. They hooked Paco to his leash and went out into the cool night air. There was only one other coach at the park, on the far side. Clouds were coming in, framing the full moon.

"That's pretty," Eric said.

"Yes," she said, taking Eric's hand.

"I'll be glad when we're out of here," he said.

"Is it gonna be better where we're going?"

Eric was quiet for a minute as they strolled. "I don't know. I hope so."

"Maybe we should have just stayed in Florida."

"Told you I'd drop you off, remember?" Eric said.

"I meant us, not me," she said. "I'm not going anywhere without you."

Eric looked at her red hair and freckles and delicate beauty in the moonlight. "I'm glad. Wasn't sure at first. Now I can't imagine being without you."

"You're looking at me differently the last couple of days," she said, eyes searching.

"You know why," he said.

"I do?" she asked, soft smile on her lips.

"You're gonna make me say it, aren't you," he said. "Fine. I love you."

She stopped, grabbing him, embracing. "I love you too, but you already knew that."

"Like you didn't," Eric said.

"Sometimes you're hard to read," she said.

"Everybody tells me that. Must be some truth to it, I guess."

"Let's go back inside."

"Okay," Eric said. He took her hand and they went back.

"Want a treat, Paco?" Kim asked. He stood on his hind legs, tail wagging, front paws pumping. "Guess that's a yes."

Eric laughed. He pulled his laptop case out of the closet.

"Would you mind waiting until the morning for that?" she asked.

Eric put the laptop case on the couch. "Sure."

"Good. Let's go to bed. I need some *us* time."

Eric nodded, and they retired to a night of lovemaking and sleep.

Hours later, Kim woke up to a distant rumble. Paco barked, and Eric leapt out of bed.

"What's going on?" he asked, looking around the coach in a groggy panic.

"Boom in the distance," she said. Then there were several more loud booms, sounding closer. Paco barked again.

"Oh, shit, that's artillery," Eric said.

"How far?" Kim asked, looking terrified.

"Not far enough," he said. "What time is it?"

She looked at her watch. "Four forty-five," she said.

"I'm hitching up the Bronco. We're out of here."

"Good," she said. "Need help?"

"Get us ready to go in here. Put away the loose stuff."

"Okay," she said, getting up and dressing in the semi-darkness. There was more artillery fire, closer still.

Eric had them ready to leave in less than five minutes, and rushed back into the coach. "Ready?"

"Yeah, let's go," she said, climbing into the passenger seat.

Eric got into the driver's seat and took off, getting on Route 79 and punching it amid the increasing noise to the east. A flash of light hit Eric's face from the rear-view mirror. "My God, that was a big fireball," he said.

"Where was it," Kim asked. "Close?"

"I'd say Deadwood," Eric said, grim look on his face.

"Oh, no."

"I think maybe we'll go all the way to Austin today."

"Yeah," Kim said, watching him drive. "Let's do that."

15

Upgrades

Brendan and Juan Carlos were deep in thought, the death of their friends hitting them.

"Think they're done yet?" Brendan asked, sitting next to Juan Carlos in the back of the transport truck.

"Hope so, dude," Juan Carlos said. "Wonder who we'll get to replace Chauncey?"

"Good question. Hope it's somebody good."

"I just hope it's *somebody*," Juan Carlos said. "We've lost a lot of men. Might be back on our own again."

"Truck's slowing down," Brendan said. It skidded to a stop on the dirt road.

"We're here, men," Captain Jefferson said.

Brendan and Juan Carlos jumped out of the back.

"Looks like the techs are still there," Juan Carlos said.

"They're done, but they need to check you guys out with the equipment," Captain Jefferson said.

"Who's going out with us now that Chauncey is gone?" Brendan asked.

"For now it'll be Lieutenant Richardson," he said. "We're got more men in training, though, so hopefully we won't have to use him for too long."

"Heard about him before he was promoted," Brendan said. "He was crazy."

"Yeah, he was, but in a good way," Jefferson said.

"When's the next mission?" Juan Carlos asked.

"Tomorrow, unless there's an emergency," Jefferson said. "We want you guys to get some practice with the new equipment. You'll be firing at remote-control targets."

"Bitchen," Brendan said.

They got on the dock and walked to their boat. There were several other boats on the dock getting their new guns fitted, and an anti-aircraft battery on the shore behind the deck.

"Expecting company?" Brendan asked, nodding towards the battery.

"They caught us with our pants down once," Jefferson said. "We don't intend to let them do that again."

The tech ran both Juan Carlos and Brendan through operation of the M-19 Grenade launcher.

When they finished, it was time for a break, so they went back to headquarters with Captain Jefferson. Lieutenant Richardson was waiting for them in the main trailer of the temporary base, worried look on his face.

"Oh, crap, what happened now?" Jefferson asked.

"Our sources just told us there are several more cutters and a bunch of barges on the northwest end of the lake," he said. "They're making hay in the sections they control. More enemy choppers showed up too. Better models, from Venezuela again. They just provided air support for a barge landing. Killed some of our land forces."

"Maybe the Air Force ought to pay a visit to Venezuela," Juan Carlos said.

"There's no *maybe* about it," Lieutenant Richardson said. "Wonder what's taking them so long?"

"Probably waiting on Governor Nelson's announcement," Jefferson said.

"You think he's really gonna do that?" Brendan asked. "We really gonna be a Republic again?"

"Yeah," Jefferson said. "We've already separated. You think the Feds would've allowed us to mount the grenade launchers on our patrol boats? They still had us in court over the .50 Cals."

"Really?" Juan Carlos asked. "You mean they could've pulled them at any time?"

"Yeah," Jefferson said. "Don't worry about it. The Administration fought their way to a stalemate. Couldn't get around Congress and the Courts."

Air Raid sirens started up, the men looking around in a panic.

"Son of a bitch, we're about to get hit," Richardson said. The men ran out of the trailer, the sound of choppers approaching.

"This ought to be interesting," Jefferson said. "We don't think they know about the anti-aircraft batteries yet."

"Should we get our boats out of here?" Richardson asked.

Jefferson looked at Juan Carlos and Brendan. "You guys think you can handle the new hardware a little early?"

"Piece of cake, dude," Juan Carlos said. Brendan nodded in agreement.

"Okay, you guys get out of here," Jefferson said. "I'll get the other crews down there."

Juan Carlos, Brendan, and Richardson sprinted to the docks as the thumping of the choppers got closer.

"Why don't they fire?" Juan Carlos yelled.

"Not close enough yet," Richardson said.

The men jumped into their boat, Brendan undoing the bow and stern lines while Juan Carlos started the engine. They cruised away from the docks, getting out far enough to see several cutters heading towards them.

"Here they come," Brendan shouted.

"Look, there's the first chopper!" Richardson yelled, pointing. He got behind the starboard gun. Brendon got behind the port gun, and Juan Carlos flipped the switch on the M-19. The gimbal motor whirred as he aimed at the oncoming cutters.

"Those boats aren't any better than the ones they had," Brendan said.

Thunder came from the anti-aircraft guns and the first chopper exploded.

"Yes!" Richardson yelled, his fist in the air. "They didn't expect that."

"The second one is almost in range," Brendan yelled. "Surprised they haven't split."

"I see four more behind it," Juan Carlos said. "Ready to take on a cutter?"

"Yeah, before they get close enough to fire on the docks," Richardson yelled. "We got to protect the other boats until they can get under way."

"You got it, dude," Juan Carlos said. He put the boat in gear and floored it, the three outboards sounding a raspy snarl. The patrol boat jumped onto a plane.

There was an explosion and fire ball in the air on their starboard side.

"Scratch two choppers!" Richardson yelled as their boat was getting into range of the cutters.

"Eat this," Juan Carlos said, aiming at the first cutter, the gimbal turning the gun towards the big boat. He pulled the trigger and a grenade flashed out of the barrel. It hit the front of the cutter, knocking a good-sized hole in the front of the hull. Juan Carlos fired again, hitting the bridge, stopping the boat. Men were diving off. Richardson and Brendan opened up with their guns, chopping up the water with fire as Juan Carlos hit the second cutter broadside with a grenade. He immediately fired a second round, slamming into the hole made by the first round, blowing up inside. The boat exploded, debris flying into the air.

"Damn, that's the ticket," Brendan said. "Looks like you killed everybody on board. Nice shooting, man!"

"The other choppers fled," Richardson shouted. He fired at the men in the water from the second boat. "That other cutter is turning. Let's go get that son of a bitch."

"Hell yeah," Juan Carlos said. He drove the boat straight for it. "In range. Bye bye." He fired a first grenade, then a second one, the first making a split, the second getting through the thin armor and blowing up inside. The boat listed to starboard as men screamed and jumped off, and then there was an explosion under the deck, the big boat flying into pieces.

"Hell, I don't think any men survived that one either," Brendan shouted. "What now?"

"Let's see if we can find more," Richardson said. "We got a full tank of gas and plenty of ammo."

"Look, here come the other patrol boats!" Brendan said, watching three more coming towards them. The radio scratched to life.

"Nice shooting, men! Over." It was Captain Jefferson.

"Hey, boss, you coming out too, eh? Over," Juan Carlos said into the mic.

"Wouldn't miss it. There are two big barges on their way across. Just left Arroyo Del Diablo, heading for the Zapata boat ramp facilities," Jefferson said. "Let's go get us some. Over."

"You got it," Juan Carlos said. "Over and out." He put the mic back on the holder. Their boat flew past the floating debris and bodies of the three cutters, maneuvering to avoid it.

Brendan laughed. "What a mess," he said. "We're gonna give them a real hard time with these grenade launchers."

"Yeah," Richardson said, "but remember that we don't have many boats left. We're gonna be under a lot of pressure for a few weeks, and we aren't indestructible. If we run into a chopper out here, we're gonna have a problem."

"Don't be a buzz kill, dude," Juan Carlos said.

"Just don't get over-confident," Richardson said. "Be careful. Be smart. That's all I'm saying."

"We get it," Brendan said.

The other three patrol boats caught up with them. They travelled alongside each other for about ten minutes. Brendan reloaded the guns. He noticed the SMAW down in the storage compartment with a crate of rockets.

"Hey, man, they gave us more rockets for the SMAW," he said. Juan Carlos grinned back at him.

"Bitchen, dude," he said.

"Keep that in reserve," Richardson said. "Use the M-19 when we're firing from the boat. We don't know when we can get more SMAW rockets."

"Insurance," Brendan said. "That's what we wanted them for anyway."

"Look," Richardson said. "Two barges. No cutters around. Let's get 'em."

Juan Carlos banked the patrol boat towards the launching ramp. Men on the barges noticed, getting their guns ready.

"Watch it, they'll be firing at us," Richardson said.

"Don't see any cannons on these barges," Brendan said.

"Probably don't think they need them with the cutters," Richardson said.

"We're in range," Juan Carlos said. He aimed the M-19 and fired two grenades in rapid succession, both blowing up on the first barge. It stopped, fires breaking out on the deck as men screamed and dove off.

"Go hit the second one, and then we'll finish both of them off," Richardson said.

"Yeah," Juan Carlos said, turning towards the other barge as it tried to move faster towards the docks of the launching ramp. He fired two grenades again, both of them hitting the target. The barge didn't sink right away, a group of men fighting back with small arms. The bullets pelted the boat.

"Watch it, men," Richardson shouted as he opened up with his gun. Brendan did the same, the .50 cal bullets mowing down the men on the deck. Juan Carlos fired another grenade, hitting the side of the barge hull, sending it flipping into the air on one side.

He came back down, fire breaking out as the men dived off in a panic.

They heard an explosion behind them. One of the other patrol boats had fired on a third barge, and it was burning. The other two boats arrived, concentrating gunfire on the decks.

"Good," Richardson said. "Let's finish these two off." Juan Carlos hit the first barge with another grenade as the .50 cals fired. The second barge was already under water, no survivors around.

"I'm gonna hit those trucks on the launching ramp," Juan Carlos said.

"Can you hit them from here?" Brendan asked.

"Only one way to find out," he said, aiming and pulling the trigger. The grenade flew, going further than the others. The men on the ramp saw it, trying to move the truck as the grenade hit it, exploding it into pieces on the ramp.

"Hit the others before they can leave," Richardson yelled. He went back to firing his gun at the fighters in the water.

Juan Carlos fired at the last two trucks in rapid succession, blowing them up where they sat. "These guns are fast," he said. "They'll be insane when we've got enough practice on them."

"Listen," Brendan said. "Choppers."

"Head back for base," Richardson said, looking into the sky for the choppers. "Full bore."

"You got it," he said, turning the boat and flooring the engines. They jumped on a plane, racing back. The other boats got the message and followed them. Richardson looked in the air behind them.

"Here they come," he shouted. "Four choppers."

"They're gaining on us fast," Juan Carlos said. "Dammit!"

"Keep going," Richardson said.

"Want me to shoot at it with the M-19?"

"No, drive," Richardson said. "Hear that?"

There was the sound of a jet fighter overhead, and two of the choppers blew up in mid-air.

"Texas Air National Guard!" Brendan shouted. "Finally."

"The other two choppers are leaving," Richardson said.

"I hear more choppers coming," Juan Carlos shouted. "They sound different."

"Apaches!" Brendan said. "Hope they're on our side."

"They are." Richardson asked.

"Why don't they attack?" Brendan asked.

"I'll bet they're trying to follow them back to base," Richardson said. "Those enemy choppers don't see them yet."

"I think you're right," Brendan said. "They aren't trying any evasive action at all."

"Those old Russian choppers are no match for an Apache," Richardson said.

"I think you're right, they're keeping their distance," Brendan said. "Those enemy choppers have to see them by now."

"They do," Richardson said. "They just turned towards the Mexican border. Probably think we're still following the old rules, and won't follow them there."

Brendan laughed. "If the administration was still in control, we wouldn't."

"Yep," Juan Carlos said. "They got a nasty surprise coming."

"We're almost back to base," Richardson said. "We ain't gonna see what happens, I'm afraid."

"Want me to slow down?" Juan Carlos asked.

"No, get back to the docks. We need to re-supply and get back out there ASAP. We got them with their pants down. Let's use it."

"Roger that," Juan Carlos said as he banked into the cove. The crews were waiting for them on the docks with crates of ammo and grenades.

The other three boats pulled up too, the men whooping and hollering.

"That was a good day," Jefferson said as he got off of his boat, walking over to Richardson. "What do you think?"

"I think if we didn't have air power this time, we would have lost most of the boats, sir," he said.

"True," Jefferson said, coming down from his enthusiasm. "So the question is how long will we have the air cover after Nelson makes his announcement."

Major General Gallagher hurried down to the dock, calling Jefferson and Richardson over. "Don't go back out right away."

"Why not" Jefferson asked.

"We've got full control of the air right now. Landry wants to hammer the enemy hard while we have the chance. We want our boats out of the way."

"They going into Mexico now?"

"They'll dislodge the enemy from the US side of the lake first," Gallagher said, "using Texas air power. The US Airforce will operate outside the US Border for now."

"We saw two Apaches follow some Venezuelan choppers into Mexico," Richardson said.

"Yeah, they followed those idiots right to their base. Knocked the hell out of them, but one of the Apaches got damaged on the way out."

"Shit," Jefferson said.

"It's okay," Gallagher said. "Nobody got hurt, and the chopper made it back to base, plus we have lots more where that one came from."

"Good," Jefferson said. He returned to the men on the doc. "Go get some rest, men. We aren't going out right away. We're going to hit them from the air. We don't want our boats in the middle of it."

"When are we going out again?" Juan Carlos asked.

"Tomorrow night at the earliest," Gallagher said.

"Good, then let's go have a beer," Juan Carlos said.

"Yeah, you do that," Gallagher said. "I'll probably join you later. Good job out there!"

16

Last Leg to Fort Stockton

Jason walked out of the motor home in the early morning sunshine. Kyle and Curt were already outside, kicking back in folding chairs, sipping coffee.

"Want some, Jason?" Curt asked. "Got the coffee pot running in the garage."

"Sure, thanks," he said. He walked up the ramp, squeezing by the Barracuda to the counter and sink on the inside wall. He poured himself a cup and joined the men outside. Kate walked over.

"Carrie up yet, Jason?"

"Yeah, she's giving Chelsea a quick rinse in the shower. Go on in."

"Thanks." She walked up the steps and went inside.

"She *is* a looker, Kyle," Curt said.

"Yeah," Kyle said. "More to her than that, though."

"What are we doing?" Jason asked. "Heading to Fort Stockton? Or are we gonna double back and hit San Antonio?"

"We were just talking about that," Kyle said. "Fort Stockton is only about two hours from here. Curt looked it up on his phone app a minute ago."

"Yeah, I knew it was pretty close."

"I think we ought to go there, get settled, wait for the rest of our friends to show up, and then take one of the pickup trucks and hit my place in San Antonio. Drive through the night."

"How long does it take to get to San Antonio from Fort Stockton?" Jason asked.

"Checked that too," Curt said. "We're talking a little over four hours."

"That's not so bad," Jason said. "If you got two drivers, you could get there and back overnight."

"Assuming there aren't any problems on the road," Kyle said. "I keep thinking about those numbers we heard. Half a million enemy fighters."

"You really believe those numbers?" Jason asked.

"I do," Curt said. "I believe the sources."

Jason got a grim look on his face. He took a sip of coffee. "If that's really true, this is gonna be a long battle."

"No shit," Curt said.

"Hey guys! Good morning."

Curt, Jason, and Kyle looked over. It was Gray and two his men.

"Good morning," Jason said.

"Want coffee?" Curt asked. "There's some in the back of my toy hauler."

"No thanks, been drinking it all morning," Gray said. "This is Tyler and Logan."

"Nice to meet you," Tyler said. He was tall and thin, with light brown hair and a reddish beard, about forty.

"Me too," Logan said. He had long dark-brown hair in a ponytail, clean shaven, medium build and height, mid-thirties.

"Good to meet you guys," Jason said. "What's up?"

"We were wondering if you'd like some company on the road," Gray said.

"Funny, I was gonna come over and invite you guys after we finished our coffee," Curt said. "We talked about it last night before we crashed."

"I'm good with it," Jason said.

"Me too," Kyle said. "Glad to have you guys with us. You were good in that fight last night."

"Thanks," Gray said. "You're going to Fort Stockton, right?"

"Yeah," Curt said. "We got other people showing up there too, but it'll take a few days for them to show. They're all east of here right now."

"More good fighters?" Tyler asked.

"Oh, yeah," Curt said. "Remember the rednecks that showed up at the Superstore attack in Dripping Springs?"

Logan's face lit up. "Yeah, I saw the video. It was awesome! You know those guys?"

"Yeah," Curt said. "They're broken up into several groups, but they're all on the way. They'll probably be the last to arrive."

"Nah, my brother will be the last to arrive," Jason said. "He's coming from east Louisiana."

Logan got a grim look on his face. "Any idea where he is exactly?"

"He was coming over the border north of the Sabine river," Jason said, worried look on his face. "I'm not in contact with him now, though. He's the one who figured out the cell phones were being used to track us. He had to dump his out in the middle of nowhere. I sent him an e-mail yesterday, but haven't heard back from him yet."

"Deadwood got wiped out last night," Logan said. "My brother-in-law lived there. Everybody had to flee. Lots of people got killed."

"They're coming in from the east too, eh," Curt said. "Dammit."

"Carthage got attacked last night too," Logan said, "but only with artillery. There's Texas National Guard troops on the way there now."

"I think I'd better go check my e-mail again," Jason said. He got up. "What time we leaving?"

"An hour too soon?" Curt asked.

"Suits us," Gray said.

"I'm good," Kyle said.

Jason nodded in agreement.

"Okay, let's meet by the gate in an hour," Curt said.

Jason climbed the steps into his coach. Kate and Carrie were drying off Chelsea.

"Hi, daddy," she said.

"Hi, sweetie."

"Something wrong?" Carrie asked. "You look like you just saw a ghost."

"There were some nasty attacks in east Texas last night. Deadwood and Carthage. I'd expect Eric to be around that area. I want to check my e-mail."

"You sent a message to Eric?" Carrie asked.

"Yeah," Jason said. He took his laptop out of the case and set it up on the dinette table. "Oh, we're leaving in an hour, if that's okay with you two."

"Fine by me," Carrie said.

"Me too," said Kate.

"Good. Gray's people are going with us."

"I was hoping," Carrie said.

The laptop got through its boot-up, and Jason got on the Wi-Fi, then went to his e-mail. "Dammit."

"Nothing?"

"Nope," he said. "I'll leave it on until we're ready to go."

"Okay, honey, I'll get ready. What do you want for breakfast?"

"Hell, a bar is good enough for me," he said. "Had some of Curt's coffee. He still has some left, if you guys want some."

"Good idea," Kate said. "I'm going. See you guys in a little while."

"Okay," Carrie said. "Thanks for the help with Chelsea."

"Yeah, thanks Aunt Kate," Chelsea said. Kate smirked as she walked out the door.

Carrie put her hand on Jason's shoulder, and pulled him into an embrace. "You okay?"

"Yeah," he said. "Just worried. Eric's pretty smart. He probably got away clean."

"I hope so," Carrie said.

They fed Chelsea and themselves, then got the coach ready to roll. Jason went outside to unhook the utilities just as Curt was closing up the tailgate on his toy hauler.

"Get anything from Eric?" he asked.

"Nope," Jason said. "Hope he's all right."

"He probably is. He's one tough son of a bitch."

"You guys about ready?" Jason asked.

"Yeah," Curt said. "I was gonna walk over and say goodbye to Brushy."

"Okay," Jason said. "I've got a little more to do. See you at the gate."

Curt nodded as he walked towards the office.

Jason came back into the coach and took one more look at the laptop. No message from Eric. He sighed and shut it down.

"Still nothing?" Carrie asked from the bedroom.

"Nope," Jason said. "He boondocks a lot, so he might not have had Wi-Fi for a while."

"That's probably all it is, honey," Carrie said, walking out with Chelsea. "Get in your car seat, honey."

"Okay, mommy," Chelsea said. Jason put on her straps and kissed her forehead. Dingo jumped on the couch next to the car seat and curled up.

"Ready?" Jason asked.

"Yeah, let's go," Carrie said. They went to the front seats. Jason fired up the engine and they pulled forward, driving to the gate. Kyle drove up behind them. Curt was shaking hands with Brushy. Jason stopped in front of the office.

"Thanks, Brushy," he said out the window.

"Thank you," Brushy said. "Good to meet you. Maybe we'll meet again."

"I hope so," Jason said. "Take care."

Jason drove to the gate as Curt trotted to his rig. They were all on I-10 in a matter of minutes, going westbound.

"This road is deserted," Carrie said.

"I know." Jason checked his rear-view mirror. "Gray's got a lot of vehicles. Hope they called ahead to the Fort Stockton RV Park."

"Me too," Carrie said. "What do they have?"

Jason looked again. "Looks like three class A motor homes, a couple travel trailers, and five Harleys."

"Wow," she said. "We've got a growing army, don't we?"

"Damn straight," Jason said.

"That's a bad word, daddy," Chelsea said.

"You're right, honey. Sorry."

Carrie glanced at him, smiling.

They settled in for the drive, watching the scenery become more arid as they went further west.

{ 17 }

Road Carnage

The RV sales lot was starting to get busy, Kelly working on his trailer when Junior approached.

"We ready to go yet?" Junior asked. Kelly was checking the air in his new tires.

"Five minutes, okay?"

"Yeah," Junior said. "Didn't you just get those put on? Why are you checking the air already?"

"Never trust RV mechanics. You might want to check the air in your tires too, you know."

"Did already," he said. "Before I came in for coffee. The salesman gave me a lot of pointers."

"Good," Kelly said. "How far we going today?"

"Fort Stockton is just under four hours if we take the I-10 route," Junior said. "Checked it on the coach GPS this morning. It works, by the way."

"Good," Kelly said. "Glad I got one of those. Unhackable."

"Did you say four hours?" Brenda asked. "That's a long way to drive these rigs, and we've still got a lot of Route 290 to get through, going through towns where we'll have to slow down. Fredericksburg and Harper, for instance."

"We could stop in Sonora, I suppose," Junior said. "Or Ozona."

"Maybe we ought to see how the road is and decide later," Kelly said. "If we're still feeling good when we get to Sonora, we could suck it up and finish the trip."

"That works for me," Junior said. "I'll go finish getting ready to leave."

"We just about ready, sweetie?" Brenda asked.

"You got the kitchen stuff stowed?"

"Yeah," she said.

"Then we're ready," Kelly said.

"I'll put drinks in that small cooler and stick it behind the seat."

"You got your gun, right?"

"Yeah, my pistol is in my purse," she said. "Expecting trouble?"

"Not really, but there's a lot of enemy fighters around. Better safe than sorry. I stuck the sawed-off shotgun behind the seat, too."

Kelly folded up the three chairs next to the trailer and threw them in the back of the pickup. Brenda went into the coach and filled the cooler. They were rolling out of their space in minutes. Junior fell in behind them. Route 290 was more crowded than the day before.

"People are taking off," Kelly said. "Wonder where they think they're going?"

"They *could* leave the state," Brenda said. "I was on my phone earlier reading about it. You can *leave* the state. You just can't get back across the border if you're not a resident."

"Interesting," Kelly said.

"The Governor is supposed to make a big announcement today," Brenda said. "Lot of people think he's gonna take Texas out of the union. You heard that, right?"

"Yeah," Kelly said. "That's gonna start a shit-storm."

They drove for about twenty minutes, watching the scenery roll by.

"Look up ahead," Brenda said. "Is that a motor home turned over on the side of the road?"

"Yeah," Kelly said. "Looks like it just happened. Maybe that's why the traffic is slower than normal."

"Should we pull over and see if somebody needs help?"

"Yeah," Kelly said. "Nobody else is. What's wrong with people?"

Kelly's phone rang. He answered it.

"Yeah, Junior?"

"You see that? Maybe we ought to stop."

"Thinking the same thing. Pull up behind me. Looks like the shoulder is wide enough."

Kelly slowed, his right signal on. He rolled to a stop on the shoulder about twenty yards past the wreck. Junior pulled up behind him, and they all got out.

"Anybody alive?" Kelly yelled as they walked up. There was a woman crying inside. "Hear that?" They ran to the front of the coach and looked in the front windshield. The driver was still belted into his seat, half his head blown away.

"Watch it," Junior said, looking around. "That man was shot."

"There's the woman, behind the front seats," Brenda said. "Hello! Are you hurt?"

"I don't think so," the woman said. "I can't get out. This thing is laying on the door."

"We'll break out the back window," Kelly shouted. "Come back there after you hear it."

"Okay," she said.

Kelly ran back to his truck and grabbed the shotgun, then trotted to the rear of the disabled coach.

He slammed the pistol grip of the stock into the rear window until it broke through, and then Junior pulled the shards of glass out of the way. The woman's face appeared. She had black hair and brown eyes, aged about forty-five, short and thin. Kelly and Junior helped her out of the wreck.

Brenda looked at her when she was out. "You have cuts on your face."

"Glass from the gunshots," she said, starting to cry.

"Was that your husband?" Kelly asked.

"My brother," she said. "We should get out of here. They might come back. They were following us on and off since we left Houston."

"I'm so sorry," Brenda said.

"Do you have a cellphone?" Kelly asked.

"Yeah, but it went flying when we crashed." she said. "Dave had one, too."

"We have to leave the cellphones. The enemy has been using them to track people," Kelly said.

"That's okay, I'm not going back into that motor home after it. Where you guys going?" she asked.

"West," Kelly said.

"What's your name, sweetie?" Brenda asked.

"Rachel," she said.

"I'm Brenda. This is Kelly, and that's Junior."

"Thanks so much for stopping."

"You're welcome," Kelly said. "Let's get out of here before they come back."

"Yes, please," Rachel said.

"You can ride with us in the truck," Brenda said. "C'mon."

"Call me if you want to stop somewhere on the way," Junior said.

"Will do," Kelly said. "You got guns up front, right?"

"My sawed-off shotgun is next to the driver's seat, and I got my piece too, of course."

"Good," Kelly said. "Stay sharp. I think the road is dangerous now."

"They can't track us anymore, can they?" Brenda asked as they got to the truck.

"I don't think so, but they might be going after people randomly."

"We weren't random," Rachel said.

They got into the truck and Kelly drove back onto the road, Junior behind him. They got up to speed quickly.

"Well, that was what caused the traffic to slow down," Kelly said.

"Sorry," Rachel said. She sat against the window, Brenda in the middle next to Kelly.

"What happened in Houston?" Brenda asked.

"My brother was one of the citizens who went into the city to fight the Islamists," she said. "He got attacked at his house later that day. Fought them off. Killed several of them."

"So he fled," Brenda asked. "Why did you go with him?"

"Things are really bad along the gulf coast now. There's been boat after boat dumping enemy fighters. They're regrouping with people already in Houston. It isn't safe there."

Kelly and Brenda glanced at each other.

"Why the hell isn't that on the news?" Kelly asked. "They're covering the riots as if they're just something normal. This ain't normal. It's an invasion."

"Something's wrong with the city government," Rachel said. "The media is afraid to say anything in Houston. The Mayor is threatening to declare martial law, with or without support of the Governor."

"He can't do that," Kelly said. "Only the Governor can do that."

"People in Houston are saying they won't comply, and a lot of the police have left their jobs to protect their families and fight the Islamists. Dave and I were the only two members of our family living there. The rest of the family is in El Paso. We were trying to go back there."

Robert Boren

"Tell us about the attack on the road," Kelly said.

"Two pickup trucks, Islamists in the beds. They drove next to us and shot Dave in the head." She broke down and cried.

"Do you know if your brother talked to the Houston PD with his cellphone?"

"Yes, I know he did," she said. "After that battle. He had to go in for questioning. I thought they were gonna lock him up for killing enemy fighters. Why are you asking that?"

"Austin PD's cellphones got hacked. I talked to them and got infected, then infected my friends. That's how they found us."

"Wait, you guys got attacked too?" Rachel asked.

"You see the video of the Superstore attack in Dripping Springs, and the battle in Austin?" Kelly asked.

"Yeah," she said, her eyes getting big. "You guys were involved with that?"

"Yeah," Kelly said. "They were tracking us. We couldn't figure out how at first. When we figured it out, we dumped our cellphones. Haven't been hit since."

"You've got one there," she said, nodding towards the cellphone on the dashboard next to the GPS unit.

"We got new ones. We don't think they can hack us again if we don't talk to any infected phones. Austin PD figured that out too."

Brenda chuckled. "We put all of our old phones on a freight train to Newark. The Islamists blew it up after it crossed the border into Jersey. They might think we're all dead now."

"You're joking," Rachel said.

"God's honest truth," Kelly said.

"What are you guys gonna do now?"

"We're meeting the rest of our group in Fort Stockton," Kelly said. "There are other groups we're joining with."

"What then?" she asked.

"We take the fight to the enemy," Kelly said.

"Oh." She looked at Brenda. "You okay with that? It's pretty obvious you two are together."

Brenda sighed. "Yeah, I'm with him all the way, but it scares me to death."

"Think I could join you guys? I know how to shoot."

"The more the merrier," Brenda said.

"Good," she said. "I'll pull my weight."

"Why do you want to do this?" Kelly asked.

"To avenge my brother, and to avenge Houston."

"You don't want to go to El Paso?" Brenda asked.

"I left there for a reason," she said. "Both of us did."

"El Paso might not be safe anyway," Kelly said. "It's right across the border from Mexico."

Kelly's phone rang. He looked at it. "Junior." He put it to his ear.

"Yeah, Junior."

"Hey, would a truckload of Islamists interest you? They're coming up behind me in a hurry."

"Why yes, it would."

"Wow, they're in a hurry. They're getting ready to pass me."

"Gonna take a pot shot?"

"They'll be past me too fast."

"Okay, I see them coming around. I'll speed up so they have plenty of room to get behind me. I need a few seconds to get the shotgun out. Be careful. Don't hit the debris." He ended the call.

"Oh shit," Brenda said.

"Hand me the shotgun," Kelly said.

"You sure about this?" she asked as she reached behind the seat.

"Yeah," he said. "I've had enough of these creeps."

"I say blow them away," Rachel said.

"Here it is," Brenda said, putting it across their laps. "Do I need to cock it?"

"Nah, it's a semi-auto." Kelly brought it up, resting it on the window sill, it's short pistol grip under his arm. "Good, they're getting ready to pass us on the left." Kelly watched in the rear-view mirror. "Hold onto the steering wheel."

"Kelly…" Brenda said. She grabbed the wheel. Kelly's hands went on the shotgun. As the cab of the truck came into view, Kelly pulled the trigger, filling it with buckshot. The truck careened onto the shoulder and rolled several times.

"Yes!" Kelly said. Then they heard a shotgun blast behind them. Another truck behind them swerved, almost losing control, trying to get away from Junior's shotgun. He fired again, hitting several men in the truck bed.

"Junior?" Brenda asked, eyes wide.

"Yeah, that truck is trying to get away. Coming alongside again. You know the drill. Hold the wheel."

Kelly watched as the truck came up, men in the cab shouting at each other, hunkered down, terrified. When they got even with Kelly he fired again, two shots, killing the men inside. The truck rolled slowly to a stop.

"See any more?" Brenda asked.

"Nope," he said.

"We're not going to stop?" Rachel asked.

"Hell no," Kelly said. His phone rang again. Kelly put it to his ear.

"Hey, Junior. Nice shooting."

"Same to you," he said. "There's bodies from the bed of that last truck littering the road back there. Truck didn't roll though, just stopped. Think they're dead?"

"I sent two loads of buckshot into the cab," Kelly said. "Doesn't do your face much good. If they ain't dead, they're close."

"Good. You okay to keep going?" Junior asked.

"Yes," Kelly said. "You?"

"Yeah, I didn't get a scratch from that. How'd Rachel take it?"

"She told me to blast them."

Junior laughed. "I'll keep one eye on the rear-view in case any more show up."

"Good," Kelly said. "Talk to you later."

"We're coming up on Fredericksburg already," Brenda said.

"That's gonna slow us down," Kelly said.

"Yeah, the road goes right through the middle of town," Rachel said. "Think they'll try to stop us because of what happened back there?"

"They don't even know about it yet," Kelly said. "I didn't see anybody on the road other than those two trucks, either behind us or in front of us."

"Look, there's a roadblock up ahead," Brenda said. "Slow down."

"Dammit," Kelly said. "Call Junior and let him know."

Brenda picked up her phone and hit his contact, then put the phone to her ear.

"Junior, there's a roadblock coming up. Looks like they want to control who comes into the town."

"Uh oh," Junior said. "Better get the shotgun out of sight."

"Yeah, we'll do the same. Be careful, Junior."

"You two, sugar lips."

She ended the call. "I'm gonna put the shotgun away."

"Yeah, you do that," Kelly said.

She took it from his lap and slipped it back behind the seat.

There were two armed officers standing at the roadblock. Kelly slowed to a stop and rolled down his window.

"Good morning, officers," Kelly said. "What's going on?"

"Where are you headed, sir?"

"Fort Stockton. Don't know if we'll make it all the way there today."

"Experience any problems on the road in?"

Robert Boren

"Nothing we couldn't handle. There are truckloads of Islamists out there. You know that, right?"

"Yes, that's why we have the roadblock up," the officer said. "You ran into some back there?"

Kelly glanced at Brenda, then back at the officer.

"Well?" the officer asked.

"Yeah, two truckloads."

"Did they do anything to you?" the officer asked.

"They tried," Kelly said. "They won't bother anybody else."

"Don't tell me about it," the officer said. He got a grin on his face.

One of the other officers came to the window. "What are you folks gonna do in Fort Stockton?"

"We're meeting some friends," Kelly said. "You might know one of them. Jason Finley."

"Shit, you're one of the men who helped out at the Superstore attack and the battle of Austin," the first officer said. "Thought I recognized you. The guy in the motorhome back there with you?"

"Yeah," Kelly said. "We in trouble?"

The officers looked at each other and chuckled. "Jason's father was a dear friend of ours," the first officer said. "We're at war and most people don't know it yet. I suspect you guys do."

"Yeah, we do," Kelly said. He nodded towards Rachel "She came from Houston. Things are worse there than we're being led to believe."

"I know, one of my friends is on Houston PD. Or was, rather."

"He leaving town?" Kelly asked.

"No, he's gonna stay and fight."

"Good for him," Kelly said.

"You folks are free to go," the first officer said. "Say hi to Jason from Fredericksburg PD."

"Will do, officer," Kelly said. "Thanks."

Kelly drove forward. The officers waved Junior through.

"That didn't go the way I thought it would," Kelly said.

"Seriously," Rachel said. "I was scared shitless."

"That roadblock is up to stop the cretins from getting into town," Kelly said. "They should have more men on it. If some of those trucks arrives with Islamists in the back, those two officers are gonna get shot."

"What should we do?" Brenda asked.

"As soon as we're past the town, I'm gonna call back there and warn them about what they're up against."

"Good idea," Brenda said. "Surprised Junior hasn't called."

"He knows what went on," Kelly said.

"Hey, something's happening," Rachel said. "Look up there. Huge crowd forming."

"We're gonna get stuck," Kelly said. "The traffic is stopping by that big park."

"This is scary," Brenda said.

Kelly rolled down his window. "Don't be scared yet. Those people are cheering. Listen."

Horns were honking all over town now, and church bells started ringing.

Junior called Kelly's phone. He put it to his ear.

"What the hell's going on up there?" he asked.

"I don't know, Junior, but people seem pretty happy about something. You hear the church bells?"

"Yeah," Junior said. "Reminds me of when I was about six."

"What happened then?" Kelly asked.

"First time the Cowboys won the Super Bowl."

"Well hopefully whatever this is gets over fast so we can keep driving," Kelly said.

Brenda was trying to get Kelly's attention. He took the phone away from his ear.

"What?" he asked.

"There's a banner being unfurled over there, see?"

"Oh, shit!" Kelly said, a wide grin spreading over his face. "He did it."

"What's happening?" Junior asked.

"Look at the banner off to the right," Kelly said. "It says *Republic of Texas.*"

{ 18 }

Overture

It wasn't shaping up to be a good morning for Kip Hendrix. The Attorney General was messing with him again, and now this.

"Dammit," he said, shutting off the TV in his office. Maria rushed in.

"Sir, both Jerry Sutton and Commissioner Holly are on the way here."

"It's okay, Maria. If the US Attorney General's office calls, tell them I'm out for the rest of the day."

"Really?" Maria asked.

"You didn't hear what just happened?"

"No, I've been busy all morning," she said, a worried look on her face. "Another terror attack?"

"Governor Nelson just announced that Texas is breaking away from the United States."

"Really?" she asked. "I remember you saying that might happen, but it still seemed improbable to me."

"A lot is happening. Things are going to get crazy around here."

"Can he really get away with this?" Maria asked.

"Well, he did it," Hendrix said. "We'll see what happens. This didn't work out so well last time we tried it."

"Last time?" she asked.

"The Civil War," Hendrix said. "Don't worry. There's a lot going on behind the scenes. We'll be okay."

"That's stuff you can't tell me here, right?"

"Afraid so," Hendrix said. "My offer still stands. Good to get it off my chest, frankly."

"That still makes me nervous, Mr. Hendrix. Here comes Jerry Sutton."

"Okay, I'm ready for him. Thanks, Maria."

"You're welcome, sir." She went back to her desk.

Jerry Sutton came in and sat down.

"You okay?" Hendrix asked.

"We knew it was coming," Sutton said. "This is gonna start a real shit-storm."

"I know," Hendrix said. "I got some pressure from the US Attorney General's office yesterday. They heard the rumors."

"What do they expect *us* to do about it?" Sutton asked.

"They want us to spy on the Republic of Texas," Hendrix said. "They'll try to blackmail me."

"With what?"

Hendrix leaned closer to Sutton and whispered. "Cecilia. Probably Erin and Juanita too."

"Oh," he said. "Crap."

"Don't worry. If it comes to that, I'll resign. Had enough of this anyway, and I'd rather be embarrassed than end up in front of a firing squad."

"You don't think Nelson would do that, do you?"

"Treason is treason, and as of a few minutes ago, we came a separate country. The US Federal Government is the enemy at this point."

Sutton leaned back in his chair, head spinning. "How'd we get to this point?"

"Us progressives shouldn't have tried to cozy up to these damned Islamists. They're like fundamentalist Christians with a tan."

"I hope I don't hear you saying that in public," Commissioner Holly said as he came through the door.

"Hey, Holly, having a good day?" Hendrix asked, wicked grin on his face.

"Funny," he said. "What now?"

"We hold on and survive until things get back to normal," Hendrix said. "What else can we do?"

"So we won't come to the aid of the Muslim population when the violence runs rampant? You know it's going to."

"Don't be so sure about that," Hendrix said. "And don't equate these foreign invaders and their sleeper cells to peaceful Muslim citizens. They aren't the same thing."

"That won't be popular rhetoric now," Holly said. "I don't view our support of the Muslim community as a mistake. Can't believe what you were saying when I walked in."

"Use your head," Hendrix said. "It *was* a miscalculation on our part. The enemy of our enemy is *not* always our friend."

"Did you listen to Nelson's whole speech?" Holly asked. "Good Lord. Damn red-necked bigot."

Sutton laughed. Hendrix didn't.

"Don't get all reactionary on me now," Holly said.

"Oh, I'm not," Hendrix said. "My comments about *tactical* mistakes aside, I still believe in the same principals, but now it's time to set that aside and put down an invasion. And make no mistake, it *is* and invasion. You hear what went down in Houston yesterday?"

"Yeah, I heard," Holly said. "So we play the Texas Patriot while the war is going on. I can handle that. Probably no other way. What about after?"

"We push to rejoin the Union, and get back to what we were doing before this happened, just like the progressives did after World War II," Hendrix said.

"Eisenhower happened after World War II," Holly said.

"You're forgetting Truman," Sutton said.

"Same difference," Holly said.

Hendrix laughed. "Yeah, well we bounced the White House between the two parties for the rest of the century, but for the most part, the Federal Government got bigger and more powerful continuously for the whole time."

Holly chuckled. "Yes, that's the dirty little secret."

"All behind the scenes," Hendrix said. "Unelected officials. Regulatory agencies. Programs that can't be reduced. Meanwhile we push progressive ideas in the schools, mass media, and entertainment. It's a long, slow process, but it's working."

"True, but we get a big setback every once in a while," Holly said. "We need to be better at avoiding them. Remember what happened after the mess in the late 1970s. Mortgage interest rates of 18% got people upset with the movement. The voters upset the apple cart."

"Yeah, and post 9-11 was a setback, too," Sutton said. "And now this thing."

"I get what you're saying," Hendrix said. "I'll file it under *shit happens*. We get up, dust ourselves off, and move on."

Holly got up. "I've got to get going. Chief Ramsey is holding a meeting in half an hour. He's invited all members of the Police Commission, plus leaders of the smaller departments around this part of Texas."

"I'm sure you'll enjoy it," Hendrix said. "Keep a cool head. *This too shall pass.*"

Holly shrugged and turned to leave the office.

"He's really upset," Sutton said.

"I know," Hendrix said. "I could go there too, but why? And I'm in a lot more trouble than he is."

"What are you gonna do to protect yourself from the Attorney General's office?"

"Nothing," Hendrix said. "Enjoy my position as long as I can. I might even chat with Nelson about it."

"Why would you do that?"

"It's in my interest to be completely open with him. He already knows about all of this stuff, remember. Guess who he'll suspect if the Feds find sources of inside information."

"Oh," Sutton said. "Right."

"And by the way, if any Feds contact you, let me know right away. I mean it, no matter what they threaten you with. Understand? I wasn't kidding when I mentioned firing squads."

Sutton swallowed, looking uncomfortable. "Okay, boss. I get it. I'll see you later."

"Oh, one other thing," Hendrix said. "Forget about going after the vigilantes. That will be counter-productive now."

"Good," Sutton said. "I thought that was a bad idea anyway."

Hendrix nodded and waved him off, then went back to an article he was reading. Maria came in.

"You okay, sir?" she asked.

"Sure, I'm fine," he said, looking up, keeping eye contact. "Why?"

"I heard some comments about firing squads."

"Don't worry about it," he said, trying to look uncomfortable.

"Oh, sir, you aren't really in that kind of danger, are you?" She came closer.

"It's a time to be careful," Hendrix said. "Don't worry, I know how. That's why I told you to put off the Attorney General's office."

"They've already called," Maria said. "They were very upset when I told them you were gone. They asked for your private number. I said I wasn't allowed to give it out."

Hendrix looked at her again, fear in his eyes.

"I did the right thing, I hope," Maria said.

"Yes, you did exactly the right thing, Maria," he said. "Really."

"I hope so," she said.

"Why don't you go to lunch a little early. I'm going to take off for a while."

"Sure you're okay?" she asked.

"Yes, I'm fine," Hendrix said.

"Okay," she said, turning to leave.

Hendrix sat at his desk, watching for her walk away, sneaking a look at her curves as she left. Then he got up and headed to the elevator, taking one to the ground floor. He walked out of the Capitol building and took the walkway to East Eleventh Street, then headed for Colorado Street. There was an air of jubilation as he approached the Governor's Mansion. A few people recognized him and came over. Reporters who were milling around outside the mansion rushed over.

"President Pro Tempore Hendrix," a woman reporter said. "How do you feel about the announcement this morning?"

"I completely support Governor Nelson," he said. "It's time for Texans to set aside their differences and pull together to fight the invaders."

A number of people in the crowd clapped. He looked at them and smiled. *Wonder if one of these guys threw the brick through my window?*

Barriers on the side street next to the mansion were up, manned by a large number of officers. Hendrix pulled out his ID and showed it, and the men let him pass. He walked up to the columned white building. The receptionist recognized him right away. She was an attractive young woman with blonde hair, wearing an expensive business suit.

"President Pro Tempore Hendrix, good afternoon. Do you have an appointment with Governor Nelson?"

"No, sorry, this is a drop in," he said. "Could you tell him I'm here please?"

"Of course," the receptionist said. She got on the phone and spoke in hushed tones, then put the phone receiver down. "Governor Nelson said he will see you now. Go on up."

Hendrix smiled. "Thanks." He walked down the hall and took a guarded elevator up to the second floor. There were more guards in the hallway, eyeing him as he walked by.

The Governor's secretary was waiting for Hendrix as he walked up. "Right this way, sir," he said. He opened the office door and ushered him through.

"Kip Hendrix," Governor Nelson said from behind his desk. "Sit."

"Congratulations, Governor," Hendrix said, reaching out his hand to shake. Nelson took it warmly. Both men sat.

"I saw you on TV just now," Nelson said. "You really support me on this?"

"I don't see that you had any choice," Hendrix said. "I know you. Very well, and for a lot of years. We don't see eye to eye on policy, and it's pulled us apart, but I know you're a fair-minded individual and a patriot. This needed to happen. I'm behind you a hundred percent."

"Well, thanks, Kip," he said. "That means a lot to me." He sat looking at him for a minute, and then laughed. "Okay, let's talk frankly. I know you aren't really here just to congratulate me and show support. What's on your mind?"

"This is sensitive," Hendrix said.

Governor Nelson buzzed his secretary. "Brian, close the door and hold my calls, okay?"

He released the button. Brian pulled the door shut.

"Okay, what is it?" Governor Nelson asked.

"I'm getting pressure from the US Attorney General's office," Hendrix said.

"What kind of pressure?"

"They called me yesterday about rumors that you would take Texas out of the Union," Hendrix said.

"Did they, now?" Nelson chuckled.

"Yes, and they threatened me," Hendrix said.

"Why would they do that?" Nelson asked.

"They want me to spy on Texas for them," Hendrix said.

"What did you tell them?"

"I told them no way," Hendrix said. "And I meant it."

"I see," Nelson said. "I assume they threatened you with the problems you've had over the last few years with your female subordinates."

"Yes, and since I've refused to help them, they're going to come out with that info. Not that I care that much personally. I don't have a wife and family to worry about. I plan to resign if they go public. Take my lumps. I was guilty of what they're going to expose."

Governor Nelson leaned back in his chair for a moment, thinking.

"I see the gears in your head going into overdrive," Hendrix said. "I know you too well. What are you thinking?"

"Maybe you shouldn't refuse these guys so quickly," Nelson said.

"Excuse me?"

"They want somebody inside. That might be useful to us."

Hendrix laughed. "Oh, I get it. You want me to be a double agent."

"Yeah, that's what I'm thinking," Nelson said. "Give it some thought."

"Shit, you're serious, aren't you?" Hendrix asked.

"Deadly serious," he said. "But I won't go forward with something like this unless I get buyoff from my cabinet and a few key members of the state legislature."

"Okay," Hendrix said, thinking for a moment. "I'm willing."

"Good," Nelson said. "Why'd you feel like you had to rush over here and tell me about this?"

"I don't want to mess with anything like this," Hendrix said. "Those guys could make me appear to be a traitor to Texas. I don't want to end up in front of a firing squad."

"You think I'd have you shot?" Nelson asked.

"We're in a war, and it's gonna get crazier before it's over," Hendrix said. "So yeah, that thought crossed my mind."

"Look, Kip, I know we had a falling out, but I still consider you to be a friend."

"I know," Hendrix said. "I feel the same way. Just wanted to be honest and above board."

"Okay," Nelson said. "Understand. I'm glad you came to me, regardless of how this turns out. I'll be in touch."

"Thank you, Governor," Hendrix said, standing up. The men shook hands, and Hendrix left, taking a leisurely walk back to his office, enjoying the trees and the sun and the smiling people on the street. *Will this last?*

Past Palestine

Too many hours on the road again. Eric rubbed his eyes, holding the wheel steady with his knees.

"Eric, you look really tired," Kim said.

"I'm okay."

"We can stop in Palestine," she said. "That's coming up in a few minutes."

"I want to get closer to Austin. Palestine is less than two hours from Carthage. Let's find something that's further from there."

"You can drive another two hours?" she asked.

"Yeah. Trust me, I can do it."

"Can we stop for breakfast in Palestine?"

"I think that's a great idea," Eric said. "We need gas, anyway."

"Okay, I'll watch for truck stops."

"Fair enough," he said. "Thanks, sweetie."

"No problem," she said. "You're worried. I can see it on your face. Carthage really got you upset."

"Well, *yeah*. I'm also worried about our friends from Deadwood."

"Did they give you phone numbers?" Kim asked.

Eric chuckled. "Yeah, but we don't have phones, remember?"

"Maybe we should buy new phones in Palestine."

"Yeah, let's do that," Eric said.

"We're getting into town."

"Yeah," Eric said. "Slowly but surely."

"This is bigger than I expected," she said. "Better slow down. Light coming up ahead."

"There's a big Shell station to the right, see? I'll go in there."

"No restaurant," Kim said.

"That's okay, we need to stop for phones so we'll be driving deeper into town anyway. We'll find someplace."

Eric made the right turn just past the intersection and drove to the last empty pump.

"I'll take Paco out," Kim said.

"Thanks." Eric went around to the pump and got the gas flowing. The station was busy. Cars and trucks loaded with personal possessions. The sight made Eric nervous.

Kim walked over after a few minutes. "This is scary. People are fleeing."

"I was just noticing that," Eric said. The pump stopped with a clunk. "Good, we're done." He took out the pump nozzle and closed the gas cap, grabbing the receipt as Kim walked to the cab with Paco.

Eric got back behind the wheel and drove slowly off the lot. "That gas was expensive. Over two bucks a gallon."

"They're taking advantage," Kim said.

"Maybe the roads are getting bad enough that the fuel trucks aren't getting through," Eric said. "Scarcity drives price."

They drove down Highway 79, which was called Palestine Avenue in town.

"Lot of hotels here," Kim said.

"Most of them look full."

"There's a diner on the left," Kim said. "Big parking lot. See it?"

"Yeah," Eric said. "Right past Mallard Street." He made the turn, and drove to the back of the lot, making a wide turn and parking along the edge towards the back. "Hope they don't mind us taking up so many parking spaces."

"Should be fine," Kim said. "We can ask when we get inside."

They left the coach, walking to the diner. There was a hostess stand in front. A young waitress walked up. "Want a booth?"

"Sure," Kim said.

"You mind that we parked our rig out there like that?" Eric asked, pointing.

"No problem," she said. "We're past the breakfast rush by about half an hour."

"You're still serving breakfast, though?" Kim asked.

The waitress laughed. "It's only 8:30. Of course. Follow me." She led them to a booth by the window. "This okay? You can see your rig from here."

"Perfect," Eric said. "Thanks."

"You folks want coffee?"

"Please," Kim said. Eric nodded yes.

The waitress smiled and walked away.

"She seems awful cheery, given the look of things around here," Kim said.

"If they feel safe enough here, what's not to like?"

"More business?" Kim asked.

"Probably. That gas station was a zoo. I was lucky to get a pump without waiting."

The waitress returned with menus and coffee. "Here y'all go," she said.

"See a lot of people fleeing through here?" Eric asked.

"Yeah," she said. "Makes me a little nervous."

"You don't look nervous," Kim said.

"I've got a job to do," she said. "Are you two on the run?"

"Kinda," Eric said. "We left Carthage early."

"It's just terrible what happened there," she said in a low tone. "It's only a couple hours away."

"We didn't hear much. What happened?"

"Islamists took over Deadwood and set up artillery. They shelled Carthage. We've seen a lot of National Guard vehicles going in that direction, starting late last night."

"Yeah, we passed some on the way here," Eric said. "We were involved in a battle in Deadwood. I'm worried about the friends we made there."

"People who didn't run quick enough had a bad time, from the reports," the waitress said.

"That's what we heard on the radio," Kim said. "I'll take the pancakes with a side of bacon."

"Oh, sorry," the waitress said, snapping out of her worried state, the chipper, perky expression back on her face.

"You, sir?"

"I'll take the same, with orange juice."

"You got it." She turned and hurried away.

"Wow, she's got that *down*," Kim said. "The happy face was back in a split second."

{ 253 }

"She's not just an employee," Eric said. "See the cook? Looks to me like they're related."

"Yeah," Kim said. "We should ask her about cell phones when she gets back."

"Good idea," Eric said. "Look. Big flatbed trucks with tanks on them."

"Wow," Kim said, watching them drive by.

"I hope Dirk and his men got out of there," Eric said.

"If they didn't, they're probably up in the hills fighting."

"I hope they didn't get killed," Eric said. "This coffee tastes good. I'm getting a second wind."

"How much sleep did you get last night?"

"Just about three hours," Eric said. "It's not so bad. I can go another two hours. We should try for Hearne."

The waitress came back with a coffee pot. "Warm-up?"

"Sure," Eric said.

"Me too," Kim said.

"Where's the nearest cellphone store?" Eric asked.

"Those are on the south side of town," she said as she poured. "You know that street just east of here?"

"Mallard?" Eric asked.

"Yeah," she said. "Take that south, all the way to the loop."

"That's 256, right?" Eric asked.

"Yeah. There's several cellphone stores there. Can't miss them. All the big ones and some independents. Which way are you guys going after that?"

"Austin," Eric said.

"Oh," she said. "Then you'll to have to take the loop northwest and pick up 79 again. It's called Oak Street there."

"Sounds out of the way," Kim said.

The waitress sighed. "Yeah, it's a pain. All the new businesses have been settling on the south side. Walmart and the other big stores are there. Kinda hurt business in this part of town."

"Sorry to hear that," Eric said.

"I'd better go. Your food will be up in a few minutes."

"Thanks," Eric said, watching her as she walked away.

"Glad we talked to her," Kim said. "I assumed there would be something further down 79."

"Seriously," Eric said. "Texas grew too fast. All the people fleeing California and Washington State in the last ten years. It's ruined small towns like this."

"Happened in Florida too, but lots earlier."

The waitress brought over the food, and they attacked it.

"Didn't realize how hungry I was for a real meal," Kim said.

"Tastes good," Eric said.

They left after paying and leaving the waitress a healthy tip, then got on 79 going east, making the right turn on Mallard. Traffic was heavier as they got closer to the loop.

"This is definitely where the action is," Eric said.

"That's it up ahead, I think" Kim said. "Which place do you want? I see Verizon, Cricket, and some locals."

"Verizon," Eric said. "The big ones are probably harder to crack."

"What did you have before?"

"AT&T," Eric said.

"Me too. That parking lot doesn't look like much fun."

"No problem," Eric said, pointing ahead of them. "There's an old cosmetics company next door. It's closed up. See the trucks parked in the back? There's room."

"Yeah, I see it," Kim said. Eric made the turn and drove into the empty parking lot. Paco jumped up.

"Later, pal," Eric said. "When we get back." He and Kim got out and walked to the cellphone store. It was deserted, so they walked out with new cellphones in less than half an hour.

"Should we take Paco for a quick walk before we take off?" Kim asked.

"It's a good idea," he said. "When we get moving again, see if you can find us a place to stay in Hearne. I don't think we should try Austin. Getting too late."

"Good, I was hoping you were gonna say that," she said, her arm going around his waist as they neared the rig. Paco was at the window, barking when he saw them.

"The welcoming committee," Eric said.

Soon they were rolling down the 256 loop towards Oak street.

"It's so nice to have phones again," Kim said, working her finger on the screen. "I see an RV Park in Hearne. It's off 485, at Vaughn Street. Want me to call?"

"Yeah, go for it," Eric said.

She got on the phone and had a quiet conversation, then ended the call.

"We okay?" Eric asked.

"We got one of the last spaces they had," she said. "The owner said it's been a madhouse for the last couple of days."

"Really?" Eric asked.

"Yeah, and get this. A lot of the people are coming from the north, not the east."

"Waco and Dallas? I know there were attacks in Dallas, but they didn't sound as bad as what we've been hearing about in Houston and San Antonio."

"I know," Kim said. "Maybe we ought to listen to the news."

"Yeah," Eric said. Kim reached over and turned it on, then used the seek button to find a news station.

"Here we go," Kim said. She turned up the volume.

"At this hour we aren't getting any news from Carthage. Lines of communication have been cut, and people are fleeing, further west into Texas and east into Louisiana. The Texas National Guard is rushing tanks and other equipment into the area now."

"Knew about that," Eric said. "Most of it, anyway."

"The problems in Houston continue to mount. After the mayor declared martial law, the citizens organized and took over city hall, arresting the mayor and city council and throwing them in jail. A new committee is running the city, with open communication to the Governor's office."

"Good," Eric said.

"Good? You sure about that?"

"Yeah, the leadership of Houston got bad after the huge influx of refugees from Katrina, and all those Syrian refugees. Changed the makeup of the city, led to the election of leftist nutcases. I saw this coming years ago."

"Rumors about the secession of Texas are swirling around Austin at this hour. No official comments have been made since the rumors started, but the Administration has warned that Texas will not be allowed to leave the Union, and that Texas must cease all actions to battle the invaders independent of the US Armed Forces."

"Those idiots have no clue," Eric said. "They caused this mess, and they're acting as if the big problem is our attempt to fix it."

"In international news, the Caliphate has expanded into Turkey, and is pushing towards the northern Mediterranean nations. The Administration is in an emergency meeting with NATO at this hour. The US is recommending restraint, but this is becoming a hard sell as Greece and Italy are threatened. The Administration has also strongly cautioned Israel to remain neutral."

"Geez," Kim said. "The whole world is falling apart, isn't it?"

"Sounds like it," Eric said.

They drove along silently, listening to the news until it looped into repeats.

"Want me to turn it off?" Kim asked.

"Sure. Jewett coming up in ten miles. Another slow down. Wish 79 didn't go through the center of every damn town."

"Don't worry, we're making good time," Kim said. "We're half way to Hearne already. We'll be there just after noon."

"Good. I could use a nap."

"You want me to drive for a while?" Kim asked

"No, I can handle it. Only another hour, right?"

"If we don't get slowed down on the way."

They rode silently until they got to Jewett.

"Talk about a two-bit down," Kim said.

"Yeah, wide spot in the road," Eric said.

Gunfire erupted ahead of them.

"Oh no, you hear that?"

"Yeah," Eric said, eyes darting around in front of him. "Look, that area over there. Looks like a park."

"Is that people firing their guns into the air?" Kim asked, eyes wide. "Is there enemy aircraft coming in or something."

"Those folks are celebrating," Eric said. "Look at that."

"I think you're right. Traffic is slowing down. Be careful."

"It's because of that traffic light up there," Eric said. "Probably the only traffic light in town." He laughed.

"Be nice," she said. "I'm gonna ask those people over there what's going on."

"Fine by me," Eric said.

Kim rolled down her window and shouted at the group of people in the corner of the park as Eric stopped at the light. "What's going on?"

"Governor Nelson just took us out of the Union!" a burly man shouted back, smiling ear to ear. "We're a Republic again."

"Wow" Kim said. "Thanks!" She rolled her window back up and looked at Eric. "There you have it."

"I had a feeling," Eric said. He drove forward when the light changed.

"What does it mean for us?" Kim asked. "Didn't expect to be leaving the country when we came here."

"It'll only be temporary," Eric said.

"You think so?"

"Yeah," Eric said. "Could be other states doing this too. The Feds have failed the country."

They made it through the town and got back to full speed. Eric glanced at Kim. She looked scared.

"You okay?" he asked.

"Am I gonna be in trouble here since I'm not from Texas?" she asked.

"No," Eric said.

"You're from here originally," she said. "They might give you a pass because of that."

Eric laughed. "Look, sweetie, if you're that worried, we'll just tie the knot."

"You'd do that?" she asked.

He laughed again. "Hell, we're headed in that direction either way. Do you deny it?"

She looked at him, studying his face. "No, I don't deny it." She had the look of reverence in her eyes again. It covered Eric like a warm blanket.

"You want it," he said softly.

"Do you?"

"Yes, but I'm not going to ask you right now," he said.

"Why?" she asked.

"When I propose, it's going to be romantic. *'Oh well, what the hell'* isn't romantic."

She smiled at him, then noticed him starting at the rear-view mirror.

"Oh no, is somebody coming after us?" she asked, fear growing in her eyes.

Eric grinned at her. "Yeah," he said. "It's Dirk."

There were two horn beeps behind them.

"They want us to pull over," Kim said.

"Yeah," Eric said. "Looks like the shoulder up ahead is big enough." He slowed down, driving to the front of the wide spot and stopping.

"Let's go," Eric said, getting out of the cab. Kim joined him and they rushed back. Dirk got out of his truck with Francis, Chance, and Don.

"Good to see you two," Dirk said, smiling.

"We were really worried when we heard about Deadwood and Carthage," Eric said. "You guys lose people?"

"Yeah, we did," Dirk said, sadness in his eyes. "We barely got out alive ourselves. Taking the trailer almost got us killed too. Had it stored on the outskirts of town. Though we were far enough ahead. Probably should've just left it."

"Glad we have it now," Don said. "Wish we could've brought mine too."

"There was a bloodbath in Deadwood," Francis said, on the verge of tears. "Half the population of the town is dead."

"Oh no," Eric said.

"Those weapons we captured in the battle with you guys helped a lot," Don said. "Can't fight folks like this with hunting guns. Not in the streets, anyway."

"We're so glad you made it," Kim said. "Where you going?"

"West," Dirk said. "You still going that direction?"

"Yeah, Fort Stockton," Eric said. "We're staying in Hearne tonight, though. We didn't get much sleep last night."

"Where'd you overnight it?" Francis asked.

"Just past Carthage," Kim said. "Woke up by artillery. We left early."

"You guys are really lucky," Dirk said. "If you would've hit the Texas border just a few hours later…"

"That keeps playing out in my mind over and over," Eric said. "You heard about what Governor Nelson did?"

"Yeah, got caught up in the celebration in Palestine," Dirk said. "I'm happy about it."

"Me too," Francis said.

"It had to happen," Eric said. "Things are gonna get crazy, though. You know that, right?"

"Your group gonna be part of the resistance?" Don asked. "You gonna fight the invaders?"

"Yeah," Eric said.

"Mind if we join you?" Dirk asked.

"I was hoping you'd want to," Eric said.

"Me too," Kim said. "Better call ahead to the Hearne RV Park, though. We talked to them a little while ago. They were almost out of spaces."

"Good, we'll do that. We could use sleep too. Only got about a few hours since we saw you guys."

"You got anybody else with you?"

"My wife," Francis said. "Don's daughter and her friend. They're sleeping."

"Good," Eric said. "Let's get going."

"Yeah," Dirk said, shaking Eric's hand. "Thanks."

Eric and Kim nodded, and they got back into their vehicles and took off.

{ 20 }

Rules of Engagement

The hallway was alive with activity, men rushing from one office door to another, the building filled with whispers.

"It must have happened," Brendan said as he walked to the meeting room with Juan Carlos and Lieutenant Richardson.

"Captain Jefferson was mum when I talked to him," Richardson said. "Haven't listened to the news yet today."

They walked into the room. Lieutenant General Gallagher and Lieutenant General Landry were both in the conference room.

"Hi, men," Landry said. "Nice shooting yesterday."

"Thanks," Richardson said. "Would've turned out differently if we didn't get the air support."

"Glad to be of help," Landry said. "The others will be here in a couple minutes."

"Did the announcement come?" Richardson asked.

"Yeah," Gallagher said. "And none too soon. You guys didn't hear yet?"

"We just got up," Juan Carlos said.

"Hard to break that night-shift schedule," Brendan said.

"True," Landry said. "Been there."

There were footsteps coming up the hall. Jefferson entered, followed by Director Wallis.

Juan Carlos and Brendan looked at each other and smiled.

"Glad to see you, Director Wallis," Juan Carlos said.

"Me too," Brendan said.

"Thanks, men," Wallis said. He and Jefferson sat. "The other crews are on their way."

After a couple moments, the other boat crews filed in, taking seats at the big table and the row of chairs around the wall of the room.

"That everybody?" Wallis asked.

"Looks like it," Jefferson said.

"Okay, then let's get started. For those of you who haven't heard, Texas is a Republic as of an hour ago."

"Yes!" Brendan said. Others clapped.

"Sorry I've been gone for a while. I was indicted by the Feds, and they were trying to nab me."

"They're still after you, though, aren't they?" Jefferson asked.

"Oh, yeah, but we're a foreign country now. We shut down all of their operations inside the Texas border. There is no power of extradition."

"Well, it's good to have you back," Landry said.

"Here here," Gallagher said.

"I trust you men enjoyed the new hardware we've put on your boats," Wallis said.

"Hell yes," Juan Carlos said. Several other men spoke up too.

"Good," he said. "We put those on partly to sink boats, and partly to take out shore installations. You'll be doing both."

"Does the M-19 have enough range?" Richardson asked.

"Effective range is 1600 yards," Gallagher said.

"Damn, that's sixteen football fields," Juan Carlos said. "We can do a lot of damage with that. Yesterday none of my shots were more than hundred and fifty yards."

"Yes," Wallis said. "These weapons are extremely powerful. We got them from the US Navy. They've been using them for years. Proven technology."

Robert Boren

"They work well on vehicles too," Gallagher said. "We've got a source inside Texas. They're cranking them out like hotcakes. Pretty soon most of our Humvees will be equipped. That's gonna give these sixth-century slugs a big headache."

"Yes," Wallis said. "Now for the changes."

"Changes?" Richardson asked.

"Governor Nelson released several war-related executive actions yesterday. He's put a temporary lockdown on civilian access to Falcon Lake and the river on either side. Same goes for the gulf coast."

"All the southern points of entry," Gallagher said.

"Yes," Wallis said. "As of six am tomorrow morning, any boat seen in those areas which aren't part of the Texas military will be sunk on sight. Do all of you understand? No exceptions. The enemy has captured numerous civilian craft, especially on the gulf coast. They're using them to smuggle in men and supplies. That stops now."

"What if the US Navy shows up?" Jefferson asked.

"They won't bother us," Gallagher said. "The US Navy and Air Force no longer report to Washington DC."

"What?" Richardson asked. "Was there a coup?"

"No, not exactly," Wallis said. "This doesn't leave the room. Understand?"

The men nodded affirmative.

"Okay," Wallis said. "The administration doesn't know they've lost control. They think there are only a few renegades in those branches that have broken away."

"Oh, I get it," Jefferson said. "That's why Nelson could take Texas out of the Union. If they can't use those two services, they can't do much about us."

"Correct," Wallis said.

"What about the Army?" Richardson asked.

"The administration still controls parts of the Army, but that is changing fast. We now have several of their most important generals on our side."

"General Walker?" Jefferson asked.

"And General Hogan, and General Stanford," Gallagher said. "There are others."

"But they still must have enough to fight us," Brendan said.

"They rushed about forty percent of the army to southern California to put down the incursion along the border there. The rest of the army is spread all over place. After the cutbacks made over the last ten years, there's just not much left. They'd have to bring troops home from South Korea, Europe, and the Middle East to make any kind of difference."

"So we don't have to worry about the US Army?" Richardson asked.

"I didn't say that," Wallis said. "The Army is where most of the enemy infiltration happened. What we have left stateside isn't trustworthy."

"So they could just waltz into Texas, led by dirty officers and men?" Juan Carlos asked.

"Yes, but they'd have to fight us to get past the border," Wallis said. "They know it, so they're concentrating on California, Arizona, Nevada, Utah, and Colorado."

"What about New Mexico?" Brendan asked.

"New Mexico is a big problem," Gallagher said. "As soon as we lock down Texas, we must go in there. Same with Louisiana. The leadership of those states are clueless."

Wallis looked at his watch. "We've have to wrap this up, men. I've got to get down to Brownsville by tonight. We have a bigger problem in the Gulf than we do on Falcon Lake. And by the way, some of you will end up in the gulf after we get a handle on this area."

There were murmurs amongst the men.

"So," Wallis said. "This is what's going to happen. We're switching from nighttime to daylight operations starting tomorrow morning. We will concentrate on taking out all enemy craft operating up in the north part of the lake, above Arroyo Chapote.

That will stop the flow of enemy men and materiel into Texas."

"Good," Jefferson said. "We're gonna have air support, right?"

"Yes," Landry said. "This will be a coordinated operation. There is nothing to stop us now."

"What happens after that?" Richardson asked.

"We soften up all the bases in Mexico with air power and the boats," Wallis said. "We occupy each of them, and run patrols into Mexico to root out any resurgence."

"How long do we expect this part of the operation to last?"

"Week or two," Wallis said. "Then we'll add most of you to the forces in the Gulf."

"How do these boats handle out there?" Brendan asked.

"Like a dream," Wallis said. "The biggest problem we have is bigger targets. The patrol boats will hug the coast and take out smaller vessels which can get into the shallows. We've acquired some larger ships to patrol further out. Eventually we'll get help from the US Airforce and US Navy, but we're not ready to tip our hand to the administration yet."

"Things are finally gonna go our way," Gallagher said.

"Anybody got questions?" Wallis asked.

Nobody raised their hand.

"Good," Wallis said. "We've got to get going. Good hunting, men."

The brass left the room.

"Wow," Juan Carlos said. "It's on."

"Yes, it is," Jefferson said. "Relax for the rest of today, and get to bed early. Be back here at 5:30 tomorrow morning."

Sheffield

Jason was driving, the miles and miles of arid desert getting to him.

"You okay?" Carrie asked.

"Missing my trees," Jason said.

"Oh. Yeah, it's prettier where we live. We're coming up on Sheffield. Need gas?"

"I'd rather gas up in Fort Stockton," Jason said. "We have more than enough to get there. Sheffield is too far off I-10, especially from this direction."

Carrie looked at her phone's map app. "Yeah, you're right. You have to get off on 349. No, wait, you can take the River Road all the way down to 290 and take that into the town."

Jason laughed. "Take a closer look, sweetie. River Road is dirt most of the way. Long haul in a rig like this."

"Oh, you're right," she said. "If you could cross the Pecos River it wouldn't be that bad, but I don't see any bridges until you get to 290."

Jason's phone rang. He pulled it out of his pocket and looked at the number. "Curt." He put it to his ear.

"Yeah, Curt, what's up?"

"Two of Gray's guys on Harleys had to stop for gas back at Ozona. They saw four truckloads of Islamists there, at a truck stop."

"Crap," Jason said. "Nobody in the town did anything?"

"They were being very discreet. They were in canvas-covered troop trucks again. Those look a lot like Texas National Guard trucks. Nobody showed any Islamic garb."

"They coming this way?"

"Yeah. I think we ought to ambush them."

"How?" Jason asked.

"We can lure them onto the road to Sheffield," Curt said. "I need to get ahead of you guys so I can get off and deploy the Barracuda."

Jason chuckled. "You sure this is a good idea?"

"Yeah. Already talked to Gray. I'll pass you up, get off on River Road, and go down far enough so I can pull the Barracuda out without being seen. You guys park on the big dirt spot off I-10 and wait for them to see you."

"You think they'll come after us?"

"Yeah," he said. "You guys can set up with the BARs, Thompsons, and AKs."

"This sounds dangerous, Curt."

"Oh, it is, but with a big payoff. More dead Islamists, and more guns and ammo for us."

"All right," Jason said.

"Good, I'll be passing you guys up in a few minutes. Slow down a little, okay?"

"You pass the word to everybody?"

"Everybody but Kyle."

"I'll call him. Be careful, dammit."

"I will," Curt said. "You too. Oh, and send Carrie and Chelsea to the back of my rig again."

"Okay." Jason ended the call and took the phone away from his ear.

"I didn't like the sound of that," Carrie said.

"I didn't either at first, but it's a good idea," Jason said.

"He wants to ambush some Islamists?"

"Yes. He's going to pass us and get off on River Road. He'll go down a ways and get out the Barracuda. We'll get off and set up a fake camp nearby, on the flat land just off I-10. Hide with our weapons. When they show up, Curt will fly in there and blast them with the M-19."

"So he's using us for bait. Great. We're gonna have to fight them with our machine guns too, aren't we?"

"Yeah," Jason said. "But you and Chelsea will be in the back of Curt's toy hauler again."

"There's no talking you out of this, is there?"

"No," Jason said. "We have to hit these guys. There might be important people in their caravan. Lots more AKs and ammo too. Anything we can do is going to help us in the long run."

"Okay," she said. "Call Kyle."

Jason nodded and called Kyle. He told him about the plan. As he was talking, Curt flew by them in his toy hauler. The River Road ramp was only five miles away.

"Should I get the guns loaded?" Carrie asked.

"Yeah," Jason said.

She went to the back.

"What are you doing back here, mommy?" Chelsea asked, looking up from her coloring book.

"We're getting ready to stop for a few minutes."

"Good, I have to go potty."

Carrie nodded and went to the closet, pulling out the two of the BARs, the mini-14, and the Thompsons. She loaded them all, getting more nervous by the minute. She left them laying on the floor next to the bed.

"How soon are we stopping?" Chelsea asked.

"In a few minutes, honey," Carrie said.

Jason slowed as he approached the off-ramp, taking it down. The other vehicles followed. They went down about half a mile and parked neatly beside each other on the flat, hard ground. Curt's rig was about twenty yards further down the road. He drove the Barracuda to the far side of it, hidden from I-10.

Carrie rushed over to the toy hauler with Chelsea, passing Curt. "The bathroom is inside the salon, right?"

"Yeah, right inside the door from the garage," Curt said. "Don't be there when this starts up though, okay?"

"Believe me, that's the last place I want to be. You sure about this?"

"I'm sure," Curt said. "Don't worry."

Carrie laughed. "Yeah, like that's a possibility."

"Do me a favor and watch out the window in the door for the troop transport trucks. Then bang on the far wall here."

"No problem," Carrie said. "After I take Chelsea into the bathroom."

"We've got at least fifteen minutes," Curt said.

Jason, Kyle, and Kate got their guns ready. Jason and Kyle set up the BARs behind a small mound on the west side of the flat area, using the bipods. Kate got next to Kyle with one of the Thompsons. The other Thompson was next to Jason.

"Carrie didn't want that?" Kyle asked.

"She likes the mini-14 a lot better, and she's a crack shot with that thing," Jason said. "It'll be okay. I was gonna hand this off to Curt again. It fits next to him in that Barracuda. Remember what he did at Brushy's place?"

"Oh, yeah," Kyle said.

"I hope these guys didn't pay Brushy a visit on the way here," Kate said.

Kyle and Jason looked at each other for a moment.

"Dammit," Kyle said. "Better than even chance that they did. I hope the old coot lived through it."

"You and me both," Jason said. "Loved that old guy."

Gray trotted over, carrying an AK. "You guys ready?"

"Yeah," Jason said. "You?"

"We're ready," Gray said. "We got our two guys on bikes following the trucks. Just heard from them. We've got just under ten minutes."

"They armed?"

"Yeah, they got shotgun scabbards on their bikes," he said, grinning.

"Aren't those kinda hard to use from a bike?" Kyle asked.

Gray laughed. "Remember the movie? The one where the robot had a lever action shotgun?"

"No way," Kyle said. Jason laughed.

"Took them a lot of practice, but they can cock and fire those things with one hand."

"What movie are you talking about?" Kate asked.

"The first Terminator sequel," Jason said.

"Oh," she said. "Never saw it. That's a guy flick."

"Yes, it is." Kyle chuckled. "I've watched that thing dozens of times."

"Men," Kate said, shaking her head.

"We're set up over on the other side of our rigs," Gray said. "I don't think they can see us from the road."

"Good," Jason said. "That'll give us crossfire."

"We'll have to be careful so Curt doesn't get hit," Kyle said.

"Roger that," Gray said. "See you guys."

He trotted back over to their spot.

"I hope this doesn't get any of us killed," Kate said.

"We'll be okay," Kyle said. "If things get bad, though, you run."

"I'm not leaving you," she said.

"If you have to run, I'll be dead," he said.

"C'mon, you two, don't focus on that," Jason said. "We'll take them with these BARs. We'll splatter them right through the sides of their trucks."

Kyle chuckled. "Yeah, if there's anything left of them when Curt's finished."

They lay silently for a while, eyes on the road.

"Look," Kyle said. "Way down there. Four trucks coming."

"I see them," Kate said.

The engine of the Barracuda started.

"Sounds like Curt sees them too."

"They're slowing down," Jason said. They watched as the trucks drove onto the ramp, curving back to take the bridge over I-10.

"Here they come," Kyle said. The enemy trucks rolled slowly up the road towards them. Then the engine in the Barracuda sped up, and Curt came flying down the road, letting the first two grenades fly before the drivers saw him, blowing out the cabs of the first two trucks.

"Yeah," Jason shouted. "Open fire!"

They all opened up with their machine guns, concentrating on the backs of the trucks as the Islamists piled out looking for cover. Most of them were dead before they got clear of the tail gates. A few shots came at the mound of dirt, causing Kyle, Kim, and Jason to duck. Then they were up again, filling the area with automatic fire as Curt shot a grenade into the cab of the third truck. The fourth truck made a K-turn, frantically heading for the freeway. Curt sent a grenade in the back, missing as his Barracuda hit some rough ground. Gray's men leapt up, running towards the last truck with their AKs blazing. Two of his men got hit by fire from the back of that truck.

Curt turned the Barracuda and tried to get closer, firing another grenade. It hit the side of the truck, blowing the canopy off, the back empty now. He was getting ready for another shot when a small camper on the back of an ancient Ranchero pickup roared up, shotgun blazing out of the front driver's side window. The blast hit the enemy's truck cab straight on. It rolled to a stop.

"Who the hell is that?" Jason yelled as he continued to fire his BAR at the remaining enemy fighters.

"I don't know," Kyle said. "But I hope he gets around the back side of these guys. They've got good cover behind the wreckage of those first two trucks."

Curt hit one of those trucks broadside with a grenade, the hulk jumping into the air, exposing several Islamists. Kate opened up with the Thompson, spraying underneath, getting several as Gray's men opened fire from the other side. There were still men behind the other truck. Shotgun blasts from the Ranchero surprised them. They scrambled out from behind the wreckage, looking for cover.

"Here come the Harleys," Kyle said, pointing.

The two bikes raced in, after the fleeing enemy fighters. One of the bikers took aim with his shotgun and blasted the slower one. The old guy in the Ranchero nailed the second one. Then there was silence.

"It over?" Kate asked.

"I think so, but stay down for a minute just in case."

There was another shot at Curt, narrowly missing him, and then the short little man with a shotgun blasted the last enemy fighter as he tried to flee, hitting him in the shoulder and head. "That'll teach you, dammit!" he yelled.

"Shit, that's Brushy," Jason said.

Kyle laughed. "That guy's crazy. How'd he live through that?"

"It's clear, men," Curt yelled. Everybody got out and headed towards the Barracuda.

"Brushy, I owe you one," Curt said, walking up with a broad smile on his face. "What the hell you doing here, anyway?"

"Those bastards showed up at my place," Brushy said, shotgun cradled in his arms. "I saw them coming and hid, then followed them."

"What did they do there?" Kate asked.

"Killed most of my customers. Except the women. They took them. Don't know where. Don't look like they're here."

"Oh, Geez," Kate said.

Carrie ran up, shoving Chelsea up the steps to their motor home. "Stay inside."

"But mom."

"Stay inside. I mean it." She shut the door to the coach and rushed over to Jason, hugging him. "Everybody okay?"

"I saw two of Gray's men get hit," Kyle said.

"Oh no," Carrie said.

"Don't worry, they're both okay," Gray said as he walked up. "They had body armor on."

"Where'd you get that?" Kyle asked.

"Rio Grande valley," he said. "Took it off some of the Venezuelans that we killed with head shots."

"Venezuelans were there too, eh?" Kyle asked.

"Yeah, but mostly Islamists," Gray said. "We ready to take off again?"

"Probably a good idea," Curt said. "I'm gonna drive the Barracuda back to my rig. See you guys on the road."

"Hey, Brushy, what're you gonna do?" Jason asked.

"I was figuring I'd go with y'all," he said. "If you'll have me."

"Hell yeah," Curt said, turning back as he walked away.

"What about your park?" Carrie asked.

"Damn cretins burned it. Rather not put it back together until this war is over."

"Well, you're definitely welcome with us," Jason said.

"I second that," Gray said.

"All right, let's get back on the road before we get caught with our pants down out here," Jason said.

"We should gather up their weapons and ammo," Gray said.

"Yeah, we can't forget that," Kyle said.

The group finished in about fifteen minutes, gathering up twenty-five AK-47s, several thousand rounds of ammo, and four crates of grenades. They hit the road again.

{ 22 }

Long Haul

Kelly could feel himself on the verge of nodding off, shaking his head to snap out of it.

"You look tired, honey," Brenda said. "Why don't we stop in Sonora? It's only another half hour."

"I'm good with that," Kelly said. "We lost a lot of time in Harper."

"At least it was a celebration," Rachel said. "Wish we could've just stayed there."

"Not far enough," Kelly said. "Sooner or later the enemy is gonna get a bead on us. If the guys in those trucks got a phone message off, they know we're still in Texas, and they know which way we're headed."

"But Sonora is okay, right?" Brenda asked.

"Yeah, I'll go along with it," Kelly said.

"There's only one RV Park there that I see," Brenda said, looking at her phone. "I'll call them."

She punched in the number and put the phone to her ear. She held it there silently for a few moments, then took it away from her ear. "Nobody answered."

"Maybe they're full up," Kelly said.

"Hope not," Brenda said. "This is a small park. Could be a one-person operation."

"Well, the town is coming up fast," Kelly said. "We can drive in there and see if they've got anything."

"Yeah, it's not far off I-10. Get on Crockett Street from 277. Pretty hard to miss."

"Call Junior, okay?" Kelly asked.

Brenda nodded and hit his contact, then put her phone to her ear.

"Junior?"

"Yeah," he said. "We stopping?"

"We're gonna check out a place in Sonora. Only a couple miles up. Follow us in. It's off Crockett."

"Got it," he said. "See you soon."

Brenda ended the call. "He'll follow us."

"Good," Kelly said.

"How many people are we joining up with?" Rachel asked. "In Fort Stockton, that is."

"Well, let's see," Kelly said. "My group is showing up. About forty people, led by Nate, Jasper, Chris, and Earl. Also those two Austin cops who've been on the run with their family, and our old friend Curt. A few others. Probably about fifty people."

"Wow," she said. "That's a good-sized group."

"I hope none of them got blasted on the road," Brenda said. "I'm worried."

"They can take care of themselves," Kelly said. "Just like we have. Here comes Sonora." He slowed and made the left turn onto Route 277, which dead ended onto Crockett Street.

"This place is deserted," Rachel said.

"Yeah, strange for mid-afternoon," Brenda said. "Something doesn't feel right."

"Look over there," Kelly said. "That building is burned out. Looks like bullet holes on one side."

"Maybe we should take off," Rachel said.

"There's people over there, see," Brenda said. "At that church on the left."

"They're sure giving us a hard look," Kelly said. "The RV Park is coming up quick."

"More burned-out buildings," Rachel said. "Look."

"Dammit, something bad happened here," Kelly said. His phone rang. He put it to his ear.

"You seeing this, man?" Junior asked.

"Yeah, looks like a war zone."

"We still gonna stop?"

Kelly paused, looking ahead of him. "Crap, there's what's left of the RV Park. It's burned out. Bunch of ruined coaches."

"We gonna stop?"

"Yeah, just long enough to turn around and get back on the road," Kelly said. He put his phone away.

"This place got attacked," Brenda said. "You really stopping?"

"Just to look," Kelly said. "Then we'll be leaving."

"I'm scared," Rachel said, trembling.

"I know, me too," Brenda said.

Kelly parked and got out of the truck. Junior rushed over with his shotgun in his hand. "Stay here," Kelly said to Brenda.

"Okay," she said, pulling her pistol out of her purse. "Take the shotgun."

Kelly nodded, and pulled it out from behind the seat. He and Junior walked into the rubble.

"Look at those bullet holes," Junior said, pointing to a nice fifth-wheel trailer.

"This just happened a few hours ago," Kelly said.

"Hey, there's a cop car back there."

They heard the radio scratching. Somebody was trying to call.

"Officer Simpson, come in," a voice said. Kelly and Junior rushed over to it. There was an officer in the driver's seat with half his head gone. Kelly touched his arm, then crouched, motioning for Junior to get down, eyes darting around.

"He's still warm," Kelly whispered. "Let's get back to our rigs and get the hell out of here."

A twig snapped behind them. Kelly shot Junior a sick glance.

"You drop gun," a heavy accented man said.

"Shit," Junior said. He dropped his shotgun. Kelly did the same.

"Turn around," the voice said. There were two Islamists holding AK-47s on them. "Say prayers."

"Stuff it, spinach chin," Junior said. He spat on the ground. The Islamist nearest him got angry and stepped towards him. Then a shot rang out, splitting the Islamist's head open. A second shot rang out, the second Islamist looking behind him in a panic, seeing Brenda with her gun in both hands. Kelly leapt on him, pulling the AK out of his hands and bashing his face into a bloody pulp with the stock.

Brenda and Rachel ran over, both of them holding pistols, looking around.

"Thanks for saving our bacon," Junior said, smiling.

"Don't mention it," Brenda said. "Let's get the hell out of here. We've seen enough. There's probably more of these creeps around."

"Just a sec," Kelly said. He went to the radio in the police car and picked up the mic. "Your officers are dead at the RV Park."

"Who's this?"

"My name's Kelly. We just wasted two Islamists. There may be others around. We're leaving."

"Wait for our officers."

"No," Kelly said. He dropped the mic. "C'mon, let's get out of here."

They ran back to their rigs and took off, heading for I-10 as quickly as they could, racing up the on-ramp.

"That was scary," Rachel said.

"No shit," Brenda said. "What now?"

"Punch in Fort Stockton," Kelly said. "Let's see how much further it is."

Brenda nodded and punched it in. "Two hours."

"We're going," Kelly said. "You okay with that?"

"Yes," Brenda said. She cried, not able to hold back anymore.

"It's okay, sweetie," Kelly said.

"I almost lost you," she said.

"You saved me," Kelly said.

She looked at him and forced a smile. They were silent for a few minutes.

"You remember when we talked in the morning? After you looked at the emails?"

"Yes, I remember," Kelly said, looking at her for a moment, then looking back at the road.

"I'm not waiting anymore," she said, her hand going onto his thigh. "I love you." She leaned her head against his shoulder. "Now don't you go and die on me."

Kelly glanced down at her. "I love you too, sweetheart."

"I know," she said. "Sorry I was afraid of it."

They were silent. They heard soft crying. It was Rachel.

"You okay, honey?" Brenda asked. "Sorry. That was kinda private. I didn't mean to embarrass you."

"You two are so lucky," she said, smiling though her tears. "There's still hope for the world."

"Yes there is," Brenda said. "There's quite a few single men in our group. You might find somebody."

"One can always hope," she said. "I can be kind of a bitch."

Kelly laughed. "That's what Brenda always says to me."

"It's true," Brenda said.

"I don't care. Knew that about you from early on. Didn't stop me, did it?"

"No," she said softly. "Still don't know why."

"I worship the ground you walk on," Kelly said. "Can't explain it, but it's the most real thing that's ever happened to me."

They rolled down I-10, Brenda finally falling asleep against Kelly, Rachel drifting off against the passenger door. Kelly fought his sleepiness. He glanced back at Junior in the mirrors every so often. He was fighting sleep as well. *Keep alert.*

Kelly's phone rang. He looked in the rear-view and saw Junior holding the phone to his ear. Kelly answered as Brenda stirred and sat up.

"Hey, man, I got to have a cup of coffee or I'm gonna run off the road," Junior said.

"There's no coffee place around here," Kelly said.

"Oh yes there is," Junior said. "I got a generator, remember? And I got one of those coffee-pod things. Picked it up at the RV place. Let's take the off-ramp coming up and park for a little while."

"Okay, you talked me into it," Kelly said. "I'm having a hard time too. A cup of joe would get me through the last hour."

"See you in a few," Junior said. He ended the call.

"What's going on?" Brenda asked.

"Junior and I are having a hard time staying awake, and we got another hour to drive. He's got a generator and a Keurig machine. We're gonna stop and have coffee."

"Good idea," she said.

"Did I hear coffee?" Rachel asked, stretching.

"Yeah," Kelly said.

"We just going to pull over to the side of the road?" Brenda asked.

"There's a ramp coming up," Kelly said.

"I see it," Brenda said. Kelly drove down and parked on the side of a dirt road. Junior parked behind them.

"We can't stay here too long," Kelly said. "We're visible from the road."

"It's still worth it," Brenda said.

"Have your guns with you," Kelly said as he opened the door. They went to Junior's motor home. He had the door hanging open, and the generator was purring softly.

"Welcome," Junior said. He was filling the Keurig water tank. There was a box of coffee pods on the counter.

"This is really nice," Rachel said.

"I love it," Junior said. "Just bought it."

"Maybe I should ride with you the rest of the way," Rachel said. "That way the two love-birds can have some privacy."

"Fine with me," Junior said. "Love the company."

In a minute the coach filled with the smell of brewing coffee.

"Damn that smells good," Kelly said.

Junior grinned. "It does, don't it? Feel free to use the bathroom before we get back on the road."

"Motor Homes have certain advantages," Brenda said.

"Yeah, maybe we ought to upgrade," Kelly said.

Junior handed a cup of coffee to Brenda. "You want cream and sugar?"

"Black is good for me," Brenda said. "Smells so good. Thanks."

The second cup went to Rachel. She went to the fridge and got out the half and half, pouring a small amount into her cup as the next one brewed.

Kelly took his cup from Junior. "Maybe we'd best be going," he said. "While yours is brewing."

"Yeah," Junior said. "Don't like being visible from the road much. I can take off in about three minutes."

"Good," Kelly said, taking Brenda's hand and walking to the door. "See you in Fort Stockton. Thanks for the joe."

"Welcome," Junior said.

"See you two in a little while," Rachel said.

Kelly and Brenda got into their rig.

"Glad we did this," Brenda said. "I feel a second wind already."

"Me too, but watch me," Kelly said. "I was really fighting back there, and this will only be a temporary reprieve."

"Yeah," Brenda said. "I'm better off. I slept a little."

"So did Rachel," Kelly said as he started the truck. "Glad she's with Junior. He was nodding off too. She'll keep him more alert."

They drove back onto I-10. Junior followed, and they got back to full speed.

"Wonder if they'll hit it off?" Brenda asked.

"Junior and Rachel?" Kelly said. "He's a little old for her."

"How old do you think she is?"

"Late thirties, maybe?" Kelly asked.

"Nah, she's in her mid-40s," Brenda said. "How old is Junior?"

"He's pushing sixty pretty hard," Kelly said. "He's the oldest of my friends."

"So maybe a ten to fifteen-year difference," Brenda said. "That's not so bad. She could do a lot worse."

"What, you think Junior is a catch?" Kelly asked.

"He's got a good heart, and he knows how to fight," Brenda said. "Stock in people like that just went up, in case you didn't notice."

"Maybe you have a point there," Kelly said.

"How we doing on gas?"

"We've got enough to get to Fort Stockton," Kelly said. "Might want to get more groceries."

"Let's get settled first," Brenda said. "I hope nothing's wrong there. I keep having this vision of the place being in ruins like the one in Sonora."

"That's crossed my mind too," Kelly said. "Some of us should already be there."

"Nate's group and Curt's group?"

"Yeah," Kelly said. "Wow, look at that!"

"Are those tanks?" Brenda asked, watching the line of big military flatbed trucks with cargo covered by tarps.

"Looks like tanks to me," Kelly said. "Good."

"Wonder what would happen if a few Islamist trucks ran into a convoy like that?"

"It wouldn't be good, I suspect," Kelly said. "I didn't see any protection for those flat beds. Did you?"

"No," she said. "Damn. Something else to worry about."

"Junior is chatting his head off back there," Kelly said. "Hope he's not driving Rachel crazy."

Brenda chuckled. "Didn't think about that."

They settled into the drive again, the coffee starting to wear off. Kelly yawned repeatedly.

"You gonna make it?" Brenda asked. "I could drive the rest of the way, you know."

"We only got another fifteen minutes, assuming the estimates were okay from the map app."

Brenda picked up her phone and took a look. "Yeah, we're really close," she said, moving her fingers on the screen.

"Surprised we aren't seeing more traffic," Kelly said. "Fort Stockton isn't that small."

"Maybe nobody is going in this direction after what happened in the east."

"I don't think Austin is dangerous."

"No, but look at what we found in Sonora."

"Good point," Kelly said.

"You look more awake again."

"Because we're talking," Kelly said. "It helps."

"Wow, there's the sign for the RV Park already."

"You never put the address in, did you?" Kelly asked.

"No, just the town of Fort Stockton," she said. "I'll do it now." She typed onto her phone. "It's a few miles this side of town. We're only a couple minutes away."

"Good," Kelly said. He yawned again.

"There's the off ramp," Brenda said. Kelly took it. Junior followed him down.

"Where do we go?" Kelly asked.

"Right on Warnock, then right on the big access road, where the trees are. Follow that down. It's the second place on the road. Can't miss it."

"There's Warnock," Kelly said, taking the turn.

They drove two blocks. "There's the access road."

"See it," Kelly said. He took the turn and slowed way down.

"Wow," Brenda said. "This place is busy."

"Yeah, looks pretty packed. I hope all our people get in okay." He made the turn and pulled into the staging lane. Junior fell in behind him.

23

Friends United

Jason had the hookups done, and paused to look out over the Fort Stockton RV Park. Kyle walked over. "Can you believe it? Nelson really went through with secession. We should call Chief Ramsey."

"I was just thinking that. You all done?" Jason asked.

"Yeah, all set," he said. "I hope we get to stay here for a while."

"Me too, but after what we've been seeing, I think that's a little dicey."

Curt had the Barracuda parked next to his rig, covered by a big tarp, and was setting the ramp up as a patio.

"Look at that," Kyle said. "If I was gonna buy an RV it'd probably be one of those things."

"Fifth Wheel?"

"Well, some kind of toy hauler, anyway. You can get motor home versions, right?"

"Yeah, but you sacrifice some living space."

"Hell, I live in the garage most of the time anyway."

Jason laughed and shook his head. "You've got a woman now. She'll rearrange your life more than you think."

Kyle chuckled. "This is how I know she's different."

"What, you think she'll be okay with your bachelor ways?"

Kyle shrugged. "No, she won't, *but I don't care.* That's the difference."

"This man is in love," Curt said, smiling as he walked up.

"Be nice," Kyle said.

"When do you think the others will be here?" Jason asked.

"Don't know. Sent an email to Kelly, but I haven't heard back. You heard what the Governor did, right?"

Kyle nodded yes.

"Yeah, we heard," Jason said. "Hope the others get here quick. Things are liable to get even more crazy now."

"I was talking to Moe. He said he's got a number of reservations. Kelly, Nate, Jasper."

"Moe? That's the guy who owns the place?"

"Yeah," Curt said. "Hell of a guy."

"Reminded me of your other redneck friends," Kyle said.

Curt chuckled. "Where are your women?"

"They took Chelsea to the swimming pool," Jason said.

"Already?" Curt laughed. "Chelsea is a real trooper, so I guess she deserves it."

"I hope this doesn't mess her up for life," Jason said. "I'm gonna walk Dingo over to the dog area in a minute. It's right next to the pool. I'll check on them."

"I'll join you," Kyle said. "What are you gonna do, Curt?"

"Set up shop," he said. "Mind if I take measurements on your Jeep, Jason?"

"Why do you want to do that?" Jason asked.

"I had an idea for a gimbal mount," he said.

Jason laughed. "Knock yourself out."

"What about my truck?" Kyle asked.

"Been thinking about that too. We need to get one of those truck bed roll bars first. Maybe somebody sells them in town."

Kyle laughed. "Now we're talking."

Curt squinted, watching an old Class C approach. A wide grin came over his face.

"What?" Kyle asked.

"I do believe that's Nate's Class C," Curt said, pointing.

"Really?" Jason asked.

"Yeah," Curt said. "He's coming this way." The three men watched as the Class C motor home parked across the road from them. A small man with hawkish eyes trotted over to them, big grin on his face. Another man followed, older with long gray hair and a long gray beard.

"Curt, how the hell are you?" Nate asked. "You remember Fritz?"

"Hell, yeah," Curt said. "You know Jason and Kyle, right?"

"Yeah, from the Superstore incident," Nate said. "How are you guys?"

"Good," Jason said, shaking hands with both men.

"Nice to see you again," Kyle said, shaking hands too.

"Where's the rest of the guys?" Curt asked.

"We split up after we left the rail yard," Nate said.

"Rail yard?" Jason asked.

Nate and Fritz snickered. "We'll have to tell you about that one," Fritz said. "Another one of Junior's crazy ideas, and it worked."

"Kelly and Junior ought to be right behind us," Nate said. "Jasper, Earl, and Chris were further back. Chris had to pick up his sister from Comanche."

"You pried Chris away from Texas Mary's?" Curt asked. "How'd you manage that?"

Nate laughed. "You got some catching up to do. Remember Brenda?"

"How could anybody forget her?" Curt asked. Jason and Kyle looked at him, questioning. Curt laughed. "She's the hottest middle-aged gal I've ever seen. Tried to take her out a time or two. She's a tough nut to crack."

"She's with Kelly," Nate said.

"No way," Curt said. "Well, good for them."

"I saw that one coming," Fritz said. "Kelly never looked at a woman the way he looks at her. He's gone soft."

"I should be so lucky," Curt said. "We brought some new folks. They were late getting reservations so they're at the other end of the park, but we'll get together a little later. Met them in Sonora. Fought with them."

"You guys have been in battles already?" Nate asked.

"Yeah, a couple," Curt said. "Anyway, we got about thirty bikers with us. Most of them are in the tent area. The others have motor homes and trailers next to the tent area. The leader is a guy named Gray."

"Don't forget Brushy," Kyle said.

Curt laughed. "Oh yeah, there's a crazy old man named Brushy with us too. Looks like a little old troll, but he's spunky as hell. Saved my life earlier today."

"We're going to check on the women," Jason said. "Be back in a little while."

"All right, pencil necks," Curt said. "C'mon, guys, let me show you my new toy."

"Uh oh," Nate said. "What have you cooked up now?"

Jason and Kyle chuckled as they left, Jason stopping at his coach to get Dingo. They walked down the road looking at the rows of RVs on either side of them.

"Nice place," Kyle said.

"Yeah, it is," Jason said. "Glad to have people showing up."

"We gonna get along with the rednecks okay?" Kyle asked. "We've had to arrest folks like them in Austin."

"These guys are okay in my book," Jason said. "They saved us in the parking lot at the Superstore, remember?"

"True," Kyle said. "We've got bikers with us too. Who'd have thought?"

"Never had problems with them," Jason said.

"Me neither."

"You look worried, man," Jason said.

"Those Islamists could send a few truckloads in here and kill a lot of us," Kyle said. "There's no cover. They could hit us from all sides. Surround us, keep us from getting away."

"You'd rather be someplace else?" Jason asked. "Nobody's forcing us to stay here. We could disappear into the woodwork."

"Hi, daddy!" Chelsea squealed from the pool. She was paddling around in the shallow end, Carrie and Kate next to her. They both waved.

"Be still my heart," Kyle said, eyeing Kate.

"Still on fire for her, eh?"

"Never thought I'd see the day," Kyle said.

"I still feel that way about Carrie," Jason said. "Chelsea made it even stronger. Wait until you two have kids."

Kyle shook his head. "I'd protest, but it doesn't sound bad to me anymore."

"How's it going?" Carrie asked as they approached the fence around the pool.

"Good," Jason said. "Two of the rednecks showed up. Curt's talking to them now. How's the pool?"

"Nice," she said. "They had a bathing suit in the store that fit me, thank God. Expensive, but better than trying to wear a t-shirt here."

"You'd get arrested," Jason said.

"Ha ha," she said. "What are you guys gonna do?"

"After Dingo's done, I want to check my e-mail. See if Eric answered."

"Oh," Carrie said. "Good idea. We'll be done here in half an hour."

"No rush," Jason said.

"How you doing, honey?" Kyle asked.

Kate looked at him and blushed. "Did you really call me that?"

Kyle shrugged. "You mind?"

"Oh, I guess I could get used to it. Why don't you come in?"

"Didn't bring my suit over," he said. "I'll see you when you're done. I got some thinking to do."

"You look worried," Kate said.

"Yeah, you do," Carrie said. "What's wrong?"

"Nothing," he said. "Don't worry about it."

Kate rolled her eyes. "We'll talk when I get back. I want to know everything you're worried about. No secrets. Right?"

"No secrets," Kyle said.

"Those look like rednecks," Carrie said, pointing to the gate. There was an old travel trailer behind a battered pickup truck, and an ancient Winnebago Brave behind it.

"That's Kelly and Junior," Jason said. "Good."

"Hey, that's the sheriff's sister," Carrie said. "The one that owns Texas Mary's. Wonder if something bad happened in Dripping Springs? No way would she have left that prime business behind."

"Chris is coming too," Kyle said, "but we didn't hear that something bad happened in Dripping Springs."

"Who's that woman with Junior?" Jason asked.

"Never saw her before," Kyle said. "She's not *with* Junior. Body language is all wrong."

"She also looks a lot younger," Carrie said. "That dude looks like a prospector from the old west."

Kyle laughed. "Yeah, he does."

"What's a prospector, mommy?" Chelsea asked.

"It's somebody who digs for gold and silver," Carrie said. "My Uncle Walt used to be one of those."

"Oh," she said. "I'm tired."

"Okay, sweetie, let's get out."

"Oh, you guys are done already?" Jason asked. "I'll wait for you. We can go back together."

"Fine," Carrie said, helping Chelsea out of the pool. Kate followed, and they all dried off.

"Look, Kelly and Junior are heading towards our spaces," Kyle said.

"Yeah, they're probably next to Nate, right across the road from us," Jason said.

"Rednecks across the street?" Carrie asked. "I hope they watch their language around Chelsea."

"We'll talk to them," Jason said. "Let's go."

They made the walk back to their rigs. Jason got out his folding chairs and set them up under the awning of his motor home. Kyle got out the four that Kate had in her storage compartment and then followed Kate inside.

"Hi, Kelly," Jason said as he walked to Curt's rig. "Hi Junior."

"Well well well, Austin PD is here," Kelly said, holding out his hand. They shook warmly. "Good to see you guys."

"Good to see you," Jason said.

"Where's your partner?" Junior asked.

"He went into the trailer with Kate," Jason said.

"His girlfriend?" Kelly asked.

"Soon to be wife, I suspect," Curt said, carrying a few beers out of the back of his toy hauler. "Want one, Jason?"

"Later," he said. "I got to get inside. I sent an email message to Eric. Want to see if he answered it."

"I'm only gonna have a quick one, then it's off to the sack for me," Kelly said. "I was barely able to stay awake on the drive in."

"Yeah, I'm barely awake now," Junior said. "We've only had a couple hours sleep in the last two days."

"Wow," Jason said. "I'm tired too, but we caught up a little in Sonora."

"Sonora?" Junior asked. "You were there?"

"Yeah," Jason said. "I know it got attacked after we left. The owner is with us, over on the far side of the park with the bikers we met there."

"We saw what was left of the place," Kelly said. "And it was almost our undoing."

"Yeah, the reason we're still alive is right over there," Junior said, pointing.

"You know Brenda, right?" Kelly asked as she walked up with Rachel.

"Of course," Jason said.

"Hi, Jason," Brenda said. "This is Rachel. We picked her up on the way."

"Oh, really?" Jason asked.

"She got attacked on the road," Kelly said. "Her brother was killed."

"Oh, I'm sorry," Jason said.

"Thanks," Rachel said.

"We got the guys who did it," Junior said.

"Yeah, we did," Kelly said. "We can speak freely around you and your partner, right? Being that you're cops and all?"

"Are you kidding me?" Jason asked. "Of course. And by the way, you guys saved our lives in the parking lot of the Superstore. I remember stuff like that. Kyle and I are in your debt."

Kelly smiled and nodded.

"Who's minding Texas Mary's?" Carrie asked, stepping over from the coach door.

"Hi, Carrie," Brenda said. "We closed her down for the time being. Chris will be here in a day or two."

"Oh," Carrie said. "I'm glad that's all it is. When I saw you by the office, I was afraid more bad stuff happened in Dripping Springs."

"I haven't heard anything from my brother," Brenda said. "He's still got his sheriff's job there, as far as I know."

"We should try to contact him, sweetie," Kelly said.

"Sweetie?" Carrie said. "Wait a minute, you two?"

Brenda blushed and shook her head yes.

"Never thought I'd see that," Curt said. "How the mighty have fallen."

The women rolled their eyes and laughed.

"Hey, I've never been so happy," Kelly said.

"Good for you guys," Carrie said. "I'd better get back inside with Chelsea. Would you mind watching the language a little while she's around?"

"Of course not," Kelly said.

"I'll behave," Junior said.

"Thanks," Carrie said. She turned to leave.

"Well, I'm gonna check that email," Jason said. "I'll see you all later, okay?"

"Okay," Curt said. The others nodded.

Jason walked to the door of the coach.

"You know, it was really nice to see them," Carrie said as Jason came into the coach.

"I didn't know you knew Brenda," Jason said.

"After I turned twenty-one, I spent quite a bit of time at Texas Mary's."

"I knew her because of the Sheriff, mainly," Jason said. He took his laptop out of its case and set it up on the dinette table.

"What are we gonna do for the rest of the day?"

"Whatever you want, after I get done checking the email."

"Maybe when Chelsea is down for her nap, we ought to nap too," Carrie said. "I still haven't caught up."

"Me neither." Jason watched the screen on his laptop as it finished booting up, then went to his email. "Dammit."

"Nothing yet?"

"Nope," Jason said. "I hope he didn't get it in Deadwood or Carthage."

"He's probably fine, honey," Carrie said. "Don't worry about him."

"Easy to say," Jason said. "He's the last of my family."

"I know," she said, stepping over and petting his shoulder. "Why don't you send another message. Maybe this one didn't get to him."

"It didn't bounce," Jason said.

"Yeah, but still. Maybe you should tell him where we are, or give him your phone number."

"We can't do that," Jason said. "What if he's been captured or killed? They might have his laptop."

"Oh," Carrie said, scared look on her face. "That's a scary thought. They could find us from an email, couldn't they?"

"Yeah," Jason said. "The message would carry the IP address of this RV Park. We can't chance it. We'll just have to wait for him to reply."

"Mommy, I'm tired," Chelsea said.

"Okay, let's get you down for a nap," she said. "Jason, could you close the blinds?"

"On it," he said, getting up. He looked out the front window, watching Junior stumble into his Brave. "Junior is beat. He almost fell climbing into his rig."

"Yeah, Kelly and Brenda looked really tired, too," Carrie said. She tucked Chelsea in on the couch. "Hope things are quiet long enough for them to catch up."

"Wish I would've heard back from Eric," Jason said as he followed Carrie into the bedroom. "Now I'm just going to lay awake and worry."

"No you won't," she said. "You're too tired for that."

They slid the door shut and got into bed. They were asleep in no time.

24

Hearne

E ric was driving, Kim navigating as best she could, both of them road-weary.

"Stay to the right," Kim said. "Don't take the big road branching to the left. That's Old Franklin Highway. It goes further south into town."

"Got it," Eric said, taking the right exit. "This still says Highway 79."

"I know," she said. "Trust me. We'll pass the Hearne Holiday Inn. Take the next right turn after that."

They drove the big sweeping curve. "There's the Holiday Inn," Eric said. "That a Love's truck stop past it? We could use some gas."

"Looks like it," Kim said. "Right past our street. You'll have to turn left onto State Road 485 from there."

Robert Boren

"No problem," Eric said. He drove past 485 and pulled into the truck stop. Paco jumped up and down.

"Not now, boy," Eric said. "We're almost home."

"Maybe I should hit the store for some food."

"Yeah, go ahead," Eric said. He got out and pumped the gas, keeping an eye on Highway 79 and State Road 485. The pump stopped with a clunk just as Kim hurried back over with two bags in her arms.

"Done?" she asked.

"Yep," he said. "Let's go."

"You see Dirk go by?" she asked.

"No, I saw him pull off at the first truck stop, right before the big curve. He'll be along."

They got back in their rig and made the left turn onto 485. The RV Park was to their left, right before Vaughn Lane.

"Turn left there," Kim said, pointing to the gate. He made a wide turn and drove up to the staging area. The park was covered with a thick canopy of trees. There were few spaces open.

"I'll take Paco while you pay, if you want," Kim said.

"Nah, let's do it together after we get settled. It hasn't been that long."

Kim looked at Paco. "Sorry, fella."

A young man was behind the desk in the office.

"Hi," he said. "Got reservations?"

"Finley," Kim said. "I called an hour ago."

"Oh, yes," he said. "Here it is." He pulled out a packet of papers and slid it to them.

"Wow, you guys are organized," Kim said.

"Thanks," the young man said.

The door opened behind them. Dirk strode in with Francis.

"There's our friends," Eric said.

"You the ones who called a little while ago?" the young man asked.

"Yeah," he said. "Dirk."

"Good, we got you all set too."

"Great," Dirk said.

"You aren't right next to each other. Sorry. We were already too full. You're on the next row over. If you want to stay more than one night, we can move you closer. Got some folks leaving tomorrow."

"No problem," Dirk said.

"Yeah, it'll be fine," Eric said. "We're gonna get set up and take a nap. Talk to you later."

"Sounds good," Dirk said. "We need sleep bad. Probably won't be up and around till six or seven."

"Fair enough. See you then." Eric held the door open for Kim and the left the office.

"Can't wait to get into bed," Kim said.

"Yeah, me too. I'll only hook up the power for now. We got plenty of water in the tank."

"Good," Kim said.

"Maybe on second thought, you should take Paco while I'm doing this. That way we can hit the sack in about ten minutes."

"Sounds good," she said. Eric drove them to their spot. It was a tight back-in spot.

"I'll have to unhitch the Bronco," Eric said.

"Why?"

"Can't back up with it connected," he said. "Don't worry, it'll only take a few minutes."

They were all done in about ten minutes, Paco walked and happy. Kim was feeding him when Eric walked into the coach.

"Just about ready?" he asked.

"Yes," she said. "I'm so tired."

They climbed into the corner bed together and pulled the curtain shut, not waking up until Eric's phone alarm went off at six pm.

"Do we have to get up already?" Kim asked, stretching.

"We do if we want to get to sleep later tonight," he said. "Up and at 'em."

"You're so mean," she said, smiling. "What are you gonna do?"

"Check my damn email before something happens," he said. "Hopefully there will be something from Jason."

He climbed out of bed and put on his clothes. Paco trotted over.

"Want me to take him?" Kim asked as she pulled a dress on.

"Give me a few minutes and I'll go with you," Eric said.

"Okay," she said. "Hungry?"

"Yeah."

"Okay, I'll get something started," she said.

Eric had his laptop on the dinette table. He watched it boot up as Paco sat, looking up at him. "Stop that," he said. "You're making me nervous."

"Who, me?" Kim asked.

Eric laughed. "No, Paco. He's trying to instill guilt."

Kim laughed. "Spam and eggs okay for dinner? With frozen hash browns?"

"Sounds really good," Eric said. "Oh, cool, there's an email from Jason."

"Really? Great."

"Shit, this is from a few days ago," he said. He read it, then sent a reply.

"He have anything interesting to say?" Kim asked.

"They're heading west, but I already knew that."

"He tell you where?"

"Yeah, in code," Eric said. "Fort Stockton."

"Is it nice?"

Eric laughed. "Nice place to camp. There's a good RV Park there. Not much of a town. It's closer to desert than here."

"Think he's there yet?"

"I hope so," Eric said. "I gave him my cell number."

"Isn't that risky?"

"A little, but we have to make contact. I'm sure he's replaced his phone by now. You at a good stopping point for the walk?"

"Yeah," she said. "Let's go."

Paco jumped up and down with excitement. They took him out the door, walking into the early evening.

"Glad it's not dark yet," Kim said.

"Will be soon," he said, looking around as they walked. "This is a lot different than Florida."

"Feels less humid," Kim said.

"It is," he said. "But we *can* get some weather. Even have twisters every so often."

"Really? Those scare me. Do they happen in Austin?"

"They're rare as far south as Austin. Don't worry. Wrong season for them. We'll be fine." He held the leash tight as Paco strained against it, trying to sniff something. "Take it easy, boy."

They headed back towards their rig. "Looks like Dirk's got the lights in his trailer on." Kim said.

"Yeah," Eric said. "Let's eat first, then see if they want to chat."

"All right," Kim said. They climbed back into their trailer. Kim got busy with dinner. Eric checked his laptop again.

"No reply yet."

"Don't worry," Kim said. "It'll be okay."

They got finished with dinner in about half an hour.

"Damn, I'm sleepy already," Eric said.

"Good," Kim said. "Let's go chat with our friends before we turn in."

"Okay," Eric said. They left their coach, walking through the cool evening. Dirk, Chance, Francis, and Don were sitting outside their trailer on folding chairs.

"Get enough sleep?" Dirk asked, getting up. He grabbed two more chairs and put them out.

"Yeah," Eric said. "You guys?" He and Kim sat.

"I'm rested, but I won't be up late tonight," Chance said. "What's the plan for tomorrow?"

"I'd love to get as far as Fredericksburg," Eric said.

"How long is the drive?" Don asked.

"A little over three hours," Kim said. "We were looking at it earlier."

"That's assuming we don't run into any problems, of course," Eric said.

"Yeah," Francis said. "Been reading some bad stories on the web."

"How's your ammo holding up?" Eric asked.

"We're good there. Captured more guns and a bunch of ammo during the last battle. We got another crate of grenades, too. How about you?"

"We still have lots of ammo for the AKs, and the other guns. Still have grenades from the battle at the grocery store too. I think there's at least twenty left."

"Good," Dirk said. "Let's hope we don't have to use them until we're ready."

"Seriously," Kim said.

"Anybody else from your group get away?" Eric asked

"Yeah, about ten, but they went east instead of west," Dirk said. "They're in Louisiana if they're still alive."

"I'm pretty worried about them," Chance said.

"Yeah, I would be too," Eric said. "Wonder how the enemy got that artillery through there?"

"Been wondering the same thing," Francis. "We got cut off from the people who went that direction during the battle. Talked to one of them on my cellphone before I trashed it back there. They thought they could make it to safety."

"Which way are we taking tomorrow?" Dirk asked.

"I'd suggest 290," Eric said. "That'll take us south of the busiest parts of Austin."

"Yeah, he's right," Don said. "Made that drive quite a few times. It's the best way."

"Well then, 290 it is," Dirk asked. "You guys want a beer or something?"

"If you don't mind, I'd rather turn in," Kim said. "I'm already tired."

"Me too," Eric said.

"Don't blame you," Dirk said. "What time should we leave tomorrow?"

"How about seven?" Chance asked.

"I'm good with that," Eric said.

"Okay, goodnight you two," Dirk said.

"Good night," Kim said. Eric nodded.

Kim and Eric walked away. Eric's phone rang before they got to their coach. He put it to his ear.

"Eric? It's Jason."

"Jason! Thank God. Where are you guys?"

"We just made it to Fort Stockton today. Where are you?"

"Just outside of Hearne," Eric said. "We're gonna try to make it to Fredericksburg tomorrow."

"I'd suggest not going by the folk's place," Jason said. "Probably not safe."

"What about his guns?"

"I got them," Jason said.

"All of them?" Eric asked.

"All the military weapons. The BARs and the Thompsons."

"Okay," Eric said. "Guess there's no reason to go there, then."

"You armed well enough?"

"Yeah, we got some captured AK-47s and a bunch of ammo. Also a crate of grenades."

"Saw some action?"

"Yeah, sure did," Eric said. "Deadwood."

"Shit. Heard about what happened there."

"We got some folks with us from there. Good fighters. They barely got out of that mess alive."

"Good," Jason said. "We've got a growing army here too."

"Glad to hear it. Think the phones are safe now?"

"As long as we don't talk to anybody infected, we *should* be okay."

"You don't sound so sure," Eric said.

"I'm *not* so sure," Jason said. "So watch yourselves."

"Will do. We'll see you in a couple days. If we can make Fredericksburg tomorrow, then it's only another three hours to Fort Stockton."

"Well, good luck, brother," Jason said. "I'm gonna get off. Need some more sleep. We'll talk to you soon."

"Okay, be careful," Eric said. He ended the call.

"Sounded like a good conversation," Kim said.

"Yeah, he's okay," Eric said. They went into the coach and sat on the couch together. "He's not so sure that the phones are safe."

"Hope he's wrong about that."

"Me too," Eric said. "We're headed for some rough times."

"Even after we get to Fort Stockton?"

"Especially after we get to Fort Stockton," Eric said. "We've hurt the invaders. We're on their radar. They're trying to find us. We'll be in battle mode for the foreseeable future."

"I understand," Kim said. "I don't have to like it, though, do I?"

"Of course not," Eric said. "Sorry to be a downer."

"I'd rather have reality than happy talk, believe me," she said. "Why does your brother think the phones aren't safe?"

"Because they were able to hack at least two of the major city police departments in Texas. They've either got people on the inside in those organizations, which is bad, or they have a way to find people they're targeting that we don't understand yet, *which is worse.*"

"So what do we do?" Kim asked.

"I made my living in Florida chasing people down by their electronic trails," Eric said. "Social media, mail servers, phone records, financial transactions. I'll use those skills against these guys. I'll find out who they're connected to, where they're at, what resources they have."

"You'll be the intelligence arm of our little band of partisans, then?"

"Yes," Eric said. "I'll teach you what I know too."

"I already know a lot of that," she said. "From my prior job. We can probably help each other out."

"Sounds like a match made in heaven," Eric said. "Let's go to bed."

"Thought you'd never ask," Kim said. "As long as you didn't just mean sleep."

25

New Ballgame

Kip Hendrix walked into his office suite early. He slept well for the first time in weeks. Maria wasn't in yet. He was disappointed. Seeing her first thing always made him feel alive. The light on her phone blinking. *Somebody left a message.* He hurried into his office and sat behind his desk, holding the receiver to his ear and hitting the button on his phone to access the message.

"Kip, it's your old buddy. We're on. I'll be in touch. You know what to do."

Hendrix smiled and hung up the phone, but didn't delete the message. He went to Maria's area and turned on the coffee machine, watching the button blink on her phone. *Good opening.*

For the first time in months there were no protesters out on the Capitol lawn. The morning was bright and peaceful. Hendrix looked out over

Congress Avenue. He could see down it for over a mile. No protesters setting up there either. There *was* a police presence, but they weren't there for crowd control. They were there for protection against the invaders, and they lined the streets close to the capitol building on all sides.

Maria breezed into the office. "Oh, you're already here," she said, smiling. "Did you have a nice evening?"

Hendrix walked to her desk as she was setting down her purse and her lunch box. He avoided leering at her, which wasn't easy. She was wearing a powder blue, form-fitting business outfit that showed her figure off well. She sat behind her desk and looked at him, relieved that he was looking at her face.

"I slept well for the first time in weeks," Hendrix said.

"Good. Why?"

"I rekindled an old friendship," he said. "One that I've missed over the years."

"Oh really?" she asked. "Looks like you have a message."

"I already took it," he said.

She picked up her receiver and pushed the button. "This is from Governor Nelson's office."

"Yes," he said. "That's the old friend I was talking about."

"I didn't know you were friends with him," she said, surprised look on her face.

"We go back to college," Hendrix said. "Governor Nelson and I were very close friends back then."

"You don't see eye to eye on much, though, do you?" she asked. "Sorry, I shouldn't be asking personal questions like that."

"Don't worry," he said. "It's not a problem. We had a falling out about twenty years ago. We weren't openly hostile, but we lost the close friendship. I think this crisis has helped us to bury the hatchet."

"Well that's good," she said. "Did you want coffee?"

"I already had a cup," he said. "If the US Attorney General's office calls again, put them through."

"Really? They still after you?"

"Yes," he said. "Don't worry about it."

She studied his face. "What's going on?"

"I can't talk about it here," Hendrix said. "Sorry."

"That again?" she asked.

"Can't do anything about it," he said. "I'd better get back to work."

She watched him as he walked back, her nerves on edge. *What was going on?*

Jerry Sutton walked in. "Good morning, boss," he said.

"Don't you look chipper." Hendrix chuckled.

"So do you, actually," he said. "What happened?"

"I met with Governor Nelson yesterday."

"About what?" Sutton asked, closing the door and then sitting in the chair facing the desk.

"About my little problem with the Attorney General's office," he said. "I came clean. Told Nelson about everything."

"You told him you will resign if they come out with the info?" Sutton asked.

"Yes," Hendrix said. "It was a good meeting. We buried the hatchet."

"You're kidding," Sutton said.

"No, not at all, and I'm happy about it, too."

"So what now?" Sutton asked.

"This stays in the office," he said, lowering his voice.

"Uh oh," Sutton whispered.

"Nelson wants me to play ball with the AGO."

Sutton looked him in the eyes. "You sure about that?"

"You know what a double agent is?"

"That's liable to get you killed, you know," Sutton said.

"Just the opposite, I think it'll keep me alive and in this office after the crisis is over," Hendrix said. "I'll be considered a patriot for this."

Sutton sat silently for a moment, thinking.

"I know, it's hard to wrap your head around," Hendrix said.

"You're right. This is a gift," he said. "It will give you street cred with the very people who hate our cause the most."

Hendrix leaned back in his chair and smiled, putting his hands behind his head.

"What can I do to help?" Sutton asked.

"I don't know yet, but I'm sure I'll need you. I expect Governor Nelson to call a special meeting about this. He told me yesterday that he had to consult with his cabinet and certain members of the Legislature. He left me a message this morning that it's a go."

"Wow," Sutton said. "So you're going to take the Attorney General's calls now?"

"Yep," Hendrix said.

Suddenly there was noise outside. Hendrix stood up and rushed to the windows. Sutton followed him.

"Air raid sirens?" Hendrix asked.

"This just a test, maybe?" Sutton asked. "Nothing's going on out there. It's more peaceful than normal."

Maria knocked on the door and rushed in. "What is that?" she asked, eyes filled with terror.

"That *does* sound like an air-raid siren," Hendrix said. "I hope the enemy doesn't have missiles or planes." He looked upward out his window, into the skies.

"Oh no, they're going to bomb us?" Maria cried, running towards Hendrix. He pulled her to himself and held her as she trembled.

"It's okay," he said, petting her head. Sutton shot him a worried glance.

"Everybody downstairs to the basement!" yelled an officer out in the hallway. "Now! Hurry!"

"C'mon," Hendrix said, breaking the embrace and taking Maria by the hand. "Let's go, Jerry."

"Yeah," Jerry said. They followed the officer down the hall to the stairs and hurried down two flights, to the lower basement. People were huddled in a long hallway on both sides, more people arriving by the minute.

Holly saw them and rushed over. "You know what's going on?" he asked.

"No," Hendrix said. "Hopefully this is just a drill, but I usually get notified about those."

"You heard what happened in San Antonio," Sutton said.

"That's not happening here," Hendrix said. "This is something else. Here comes Governor Nelson."

"Kip, Holly, follow me," Nelson said as he rushed by. They followed him through the long hall, and down a third flight of stairs, officers standing by the stairwell door after they went through.

"Sorry, miss, you have to wait outside," an officer said to Maria.

"Don't worry, you'll be okay," Hendrix said, letting go of her hand. He looked at Sutton. "Make sure she's safe."

"Yes sir," he said, taking Maria by the arm and leading her to a room off to the left. Others were flooding into that room after them.

Governor Nelson called out. "Everybody come into the situation room, please."

The room filled up with the leadership of the Texas Government in less than a minute. Nelson's secretary switched on the TV behind the massive meeting table. The picture came on. Wreckage of a huge city, smoke rising into the air, fires burning everywhere.

"That's New York Harbor!" Hendrix said.

"Yes, Kip," Nelson said, on the verge of tears. "Somebody floated a nuclear device into the harbor and lit it off. The lower end of Manhattan and a big part of New Jersey are gone."

"My God," Hendrix said, sitting down, his heart pounding. "Are we in danger of an attack here?"

"We don't know," Nelson said. "This is a precaution, just in case. We don't know who did this or why."

"I've got a pretty good idea," Chief Ramsey said.

{ 26 }

Clubhouse

Kelly woke with a start, as car horns sounded towards the front of the Fort Stockton RV Park. He sat up quickly, heart pounding.

"Oh no, are we under attack?" Brenda asked. She sat up and looked around in a panic.

"I don't hear any gunshots," Kelly said, leaping out of bed. He pulled on his clothes and grabbed his pistol and rifle. "C'mon."

Brenda was pulling on her jeans and blouse. She picked up her pistol and stuck it in her waist band.

The honking stopped as they ran outside. Curt, Jason, and Carrie were there, looking towards the front of the park. Kyle and Kate rushed over. Nate came out of his rig with Fritz.

"What's going on?" Kelly asked, looking around.

People were heading towards the clubhouse, many of them openly weeping.

"Something bad happened," Brenda said.

"Yeah, I think you're right," Carrie said. She looked at Jason. "I'll get Chelsea."

"You do that," Jason said. "I'm going to grab the mini-14."

"What are we doing?" Nate asked.

"Let's go down to the clubhouse," Curt said. "That's where everybody's heading."

"Yeah, let's go there," Junior said. He took Rachel's hand. She gave him a look, but stayed with him as he started towards the clubhouse.

"C'mon," Kelly said. The rest of the group started towards the clubhouse, Carrie and Jason caught up, Chelsea in Carrie's arms.

"Everybody's coming," Kelly said. "Look at all the people. Probably won't all fit inside."

Gray and Brushy saw Curt and rushed over. "You know what's going on?" Brushy asked.

"No," Curt said. "These are those friends I talked about. Kelly and Brenda, Nate, and Fritz. Junior and Rachel. Guys, these are the folks we were with back in Sonora. We fought the Islamists together."

"Mighty nice to meet you," Kelly said. The others nodded as they made their way to the clubhouse. It was packed with people. There was a huge flat-screen TV up on the wall, showing CNN video of devastation.

"Is that New York?" Brenda asked, eyes tearing up.

"Sure looks like it," Kelly said.

"Son of a bitch," Curt said, looking at the fires, smoke and broken buildings.

The announcer came on, but the sound was too low to hear. Moe got up front on a bench and held up his hands. He was a big, overweight man, balding, with a long beard, dark brown with streaks of gray. "Hey, folks, keep it down. I'll turn the sound up."

"News coming out of New York City is sketchy at best," said the announcer. "The incident happened just over an hour ago. All cities are now locking down their ports to incoming vessels, and searching all boats already in their harbors."

"Shit, somebody floated a nuke into the harbor," Jason said, face red with anger.

"What happened, daddy?" Chelsea asked, fear in her eyes.

"An explosion, but it was far, far away, honey," Carrie said. "It can't hurt you here."

"This just in," the announcer said. "Another device has gone off in Puget Sound, near Seattle, Washington. It appears to be a larger device than the one detonated in New York harbor."

There was a collective groan in the room, some people openly weeping.

"We're in it now," Nate said.

"Yep," Curt said. "You know damn well who did this."

"Seattle police are working out a way to evacuate as many people as possible. Prevailing winds will probably blow the fallout east, which is going to make evacuations more difficult."

"Those poor people," Kate said, tears running down her cheeks. Kyle pulled her close, a stoic look on his face.

"This won't stand," Nate said, determination in his voice.

"No, it won't," Gray said. His people were gathering around him now.

"What are we gonna do?" Brenda asked, clinging to Kelly.

"Kick some ass," Kelly said.

"Yeah," Nate said. "There's half a million of these slugs in Texas. It's a target-rich environment."

"The blast in New York harbor has caused tremendous damage in lower Manhattan, Brooklyn, and Jersey City. There are no estimates of casualties there, but the numbers will be horrendous, as will the economic impact."

"The blast in Seattle might have been bigger, but I'll bet a lot more people got killed in New York,"

Nate said, shaking his head. He was trembling with anger.

"If there were two attacks like this, there's probably more coming," Kyle said. "Glad we're not in a coastal city."

"Anything along Big Muddy might be vulnerable too," Junior said.

"Yeah, and the Great Lakes that butt up against Canada," Brushy said. "They're even more lax about who they let in than we are."

"You're right about that," Kelly said.

"The White House has just released a statement," the announcer said. *"We know who made these attacks possible, and they will pay a heavy price."*

"The way I see it, this was at least partially their fault," Curt said.

"Be careful," Kelly said. "I don't like the Prez, but he didn't do this."

"He's not our president anymore anyway," Jason said. "We're a Republic again, remember?"

"Wonder if that's going to stand after this?" Kyle asked.

"Probably," Nate said.

A huge explosion went off, some distance away. Everybody jerked their heads toward it.

"What the hell was that?" Curt asked.

The popping of gunfire floated through the air towards them.

"Holy shit," Gray said. "How close is that?"

"Clancy," Moe shouted. "Get up on the roof with the binoculars and see what that is."

A scraggly rail of a man nodded, grabbed the binoculars out of a cabinet by the door, and rushed out, scrambling up the lattice to the roof. Kelly, Nate, and Junior ran outside, followed by Gray and his men, Brushy, Jason, Curt, and Kyle.

"Attack on a military convoy," Clancy shouted. "On eastbound I-10, maybe half a mile away. They blew up one of the tanks. Looks like they're trying to steal the others. They aren't getting much resistance."

"Yet," Curt said, running towards his rig.

"I know what he's gonna do," Kyle said. "Jason, let's go get the BARs."

"Way ahead of you," Jason said.

"We're going too," Gray's men said. Kelly, Nate, and Junior nodded, rushing behind them.

Kate, Carrie, Brenda, and Rachel stood watching their men run away.

"Dammit," Kate said. "Should we go after them?"

"No, let them do this," Brenda said. "But let's go get our rigs ready to roll. I have a feeling we won't be staying here long."

"Curt is gonna ruin their whole day in a few minutes," Carrie said.

"Yeah, he is," Brushy said, hobbling over.

"Why?" Clancy asked as he came off the roof.

"He's got a dune buggy with an automatic grenade launcher mounted on top. Saw that damn thing in action at my park in Sonora."

"My husband and his buddy have BARs too," Carrie said. "You think we ought to go get the Thompsons out?"

"Yeah, let's get them loaded before we get the rigs ready."

The sound of engines starting spread through the RV Park as the gunfire on I-10 slowed.

Brushy snickered. "The Islamists think they're home free. I'm gonna go saddle up." He hobbled towards his space.

Kate and Carrie looked at each other, then at Brenda and Rachel. They hurried back to their rigs.

{ 27 }

Venezuela

It was late afternoon, Juan Carlos and Brendan getting ready to board their boat. The other crews were getting ready too. Lieutenant Richardson ran to the dock.

"Change of plans, men," he yelled. "Get your butts to headquarters for a briefing right now."

"What now, dude?" Juan Carlos asked.

"Don't know, but it's something big," Brendan said. They rushed to the headquarters building and were ushered into the conference room. The TV screen was on, showing CNN.

"What the hell is going on?" Juan Carlos asked, looking at the screen.

"Somebody floated nukes into New York Harbor and Puget Sound," Captain Jefferson said.

"No," Juan Carlos said. "My uncle lives in Jersey."

"Dammit," Brendan said. "Who did it?"

"They ain't saying yet," Jefferson said. "But three guesses."

"Something else just happened," Richardson said. "Turn that up."

Jefferson nodded and grabbed the remote.

"This just in," the announcer said. *"The Port of Vladivostok in Russia has just been hit. The device was larger than the New York bomb. It appears to have been the size of the device detonated earlier today in Puget Sound."*

"Well, it's not just us," Brendan said.

"Shit, hope this doesn't touch off a nuke exchange between us and Russia," Richardson said.

"Oh, *hell,* dude," Juan Carlos said, looking up at the ceiling.

"Settle down, Juan Carlos," Jefferson said. "I wouldn't expect any ICBMs to be flying into Falcon Lake."

"Ladies and gentlemen, we have yet another report of an attack, this time in Charleston Harbor," the announcer said.

"Son of a bitch," Jefferson said.

"Why are we hanging around here?" Brendan asked, face turning red. "Why aren't we out pounding the bad guys extra frigging hard?"

"Yeah, dude, let's go get us some," Juan Carlos said.

"Gallagher asked us to stand down for a little while," he said. "They're still patrolling the area with attack helicopters. Don't want to risk hitting any of us."

"Did he know about this?" Juan Carlos asked.

"Yeah, he's the one who told me to turn on the TV and round you guys up. Sit tight. We'll get some food brought in. Relax."

"Relax with this going on?" Brendan asked, eyes tearing up now.

"Seriously, dude," Juan Carlos said.

"Russia has warned China to move its forces away from North Korean border within twenty-four hours, or risk losing them," the announcer said. *"China responded by asking for the UN to take up the matter tonight. The US government has said it will strike quickly, and has told China that it agrees with Russia and will not be deterred by China or the UN in this matter."*

"About frigging time," Richardson said. "Let's go get 'em."

"North Korea is involved with this?" Juan Carlos asked.

"They probably supplied the nukes," Jefferson said. "We can tell the source pretty easily after a blast."

"The FBI is continuing to look at suspicious freighters in US harbors at this hour," the announcer said. *"No official word yet on the identity of the people apprehended at the site of the Baltimore device. The president and key government officials have been moved to safe locations due to that incident."*

"They tried in Baltimore too?" Brendan asked. "That would have nailed DC too."

"Yep," Richardson said.

"This is crazy," Juan Carlos said. "You don't think they'd float anything like that on Falcon Lake, do you?"

"Nah," Jefferson said. "Not enough people to kill around here, and they need the entry point."

"This just in. A small device was just detonated in Ventura, California. This is a harbor that was not considered a threat, so now all of the municipalities with small harbors are on alert, and are searching all boats."

"You were saying?" Juan Carlos said.

"That's different," Jefferson said. "You ever been to Ventura?"

"No," Juan Carlos said.

"It's really two cities, Ventura and Oxnard. Huge population."

"Define huge," Juan Carlos said.

"It's about the size of Corpus Christi," Richardson said, eyes still glued to the TV screen. "Pretty similar in most ways, actually. If I were in Corpus Christi, I'd be getting the hell out."

"We have received a statement from the White House that retaliation has started, and will be working its way from the closest perpetrators outward. Venezuela has just been rocked by nuclear attacks in all of its ports and all of its major population centers."

"Holy shit," Brendan said. "That's close."

"Not that close, but we're liable to see a reaction," Richardson said.

"Yeah," Jefferson said. "Wonder if they still want us to stand down?"

"Let's go kick some ass, dude," Juan Carlos said. "It's driving me crazy sitting this out. There's still hundreds of these creeps out there."

"No! We have to wait until Gallagher says we can go," Jefferson said. "Don't worry, you'll get your chance."

"The Cities of Ventura and Oxnard have sustained large loss of life and catastrophic damage. The prevailing wind is to the east, which will cause

problems for the rich agricultural area that lies in that direction. Authorities have said they will require evacuation of people as far east as Simi Valley due to the fallout danger. There are also plans to evacuate the nearby communities of Thousand Oaks and Agoura. At this time, it appears that the nearest big population areas up and down the coast will survive and not need evacuation. These communities include Santa Barbara to the north and the cities along Santa Monica Bay to the south."

"You sure the fallout from Venezuela won't get this far?" Brendan asked.

"Look at the map, kid," Jefferson said. "It's a long, long way from here. I'd worry more about the reaction of the Venezuelan troops just south of the border. They're liable to go crazy since we just took their homes and families away from them."

"In other news," the announcer continued, "Russia has started using the same strategy in their country to take out the radical Islamists, which is to take out the closest bases first, and then expand outward. They have chosen not to use nuclear weapons near their country. They are using scorched earth eradication in areas of their country that are linked to the device in Vladivostok. At the current hour, they have leveled all mosques in Chechnya, and are searching house to house for Islamist leaders in

that province. The UN and Amnesty International are already protesting the actions."

"Boo friggin hoo," Juan Carlos said.

"Seriously," Brendan said.

"Breaking news," the announcer said. "A device has been located in the San Francisco Bay area, on a large private yacht. There is a manhunt going on right now to find the perpetrators. The owners of the yacht were found below deck. All of them were murdered."

"We're learning fast," Richardson said.

"The odds are still against us," Jefferson said. "There are thousands of boats in each of the larger marinas."

"This was actually a smart strategy," Richardson said.

"How so?" Brendan asked.

Jefferson nodded in agreement to Richardson. "We've probably been looking at container ships. Commercial. I'll bet we haven't looked at private pleasure craft until today."

"Wonder if it was pleasure craft in New York and Seattle?" Juan Carlos asked.

"Probably," Jefferson said. "When's this gonna end? The world is on fire."

CNN was silently moving through video clips of all the attack zones. Fire, smoke, broken buildings, bodies in the streets. There was a hush in the room as all of the men watched.

"The world will never be the same," Brendan said.

"I know, dude," Juan Carlos said. "So many people have died tonight."

"The White House has announced a press conference for 9:00 PM EST tonight," the announcer said. "And it is expected that the Russian president will join him for part of the briefing."

"Good," Jefferson said. "I don't like the guy much, but we have to pull together now."

"Here here," said somebody in the back of the room.

"Provided he didn't know about it," Richardson said quietly. Jefferson shot him a glance and shook his head no.

"Something is about to happen, dude," Juan Carlos said, watching the screen as the announcers sat up in their seats, looking at notes.

"We have received a video from an Islamist leader in Iraq," said the male commentator. "It arrived on YouTube less than half an hour ago."

"We bring it to you now, uncut," the woman said.

The video showed an old Islamist leader in traditional white garb, sitting in front of the black and white flag of his army. There were men dressed in black flanking him, holding AK-47s.

"Islamist thug leader," Brendan said. "What a shock. Glad he's not here. At least we don't have to smell him."

"Seriously, dude," Juan Carlos said.

"Quiet," Jefferson said.

The old man talked, a translator's voice coming in on the soundtrack.

"By the grace of Allah, I am here to announce a new Caliphate. We have taken the battle to the Infidel in every corner of the western world, and we have just begun. Truly all praise belongs to Allah. We and our partners have placed agents in every corner of your free societies, and will use your own laws to bring you under the control of Allah and Muhammad (peace and blessings be upon him) His slave and Messenger. I have been declared the new Caliph of the global Islamic State."

"Stuff it," Brendan said. "We'll see you in hell, you sixth-century pig."

"Quiet," Jefferson said again.

The Caliph continued.

"The peoples of the world will agree that they will submit to Allah, or accept dhimmi status. The attacks will not stop, as you are not yet convinced that you cannot defeat Allah and his armies.... Allah willing, and nothing is too great for Allah."

The video ended abruptly.

"Did the government just censor this guy?" Brendan asked.

"Kinda looks like it," Jefferson said.

The commentators came back on the screen.

"We now take you to the White House," the *woman commentator said.*

The screen displayed a briefing room with an empty podium. The presidential seal was on the front of it, and there were flags on either side.

"That's a secure location," Jefferson said. "Not the White House."

"Good," Richardson said. "I wouldn't want them in the White House right now. Too big of a target."

"Here he comes," Jefferson said. The screen showed the President walking up to the podium. He had a somber look on his face.

"Good evening, ladies and gentlemen. I won't recount what has happened over the last twenty-four hours, as I'm sure all of you have been following the news. The United States, the EU, and the Russian Federation are cooperating on a level not seen since the Second World War to settle this matter and bring the guilty parties to justice. And make no mistake, our response will not be a restrained series of police actions. These attacks are acts of war, and will be treated as such. We will use our most terrible

weapons, and fight as if our very survival is at stake, because it is."

"A few words about moderate Muslims," the President continued. "There is no cause and no excuse to punish the moderate Muslims due to the actions of these radicals. Remember that moderate Muslims living in our cities have been killed in these attacks, right alongside people of every other faith. That being said, the United States is not going to have the resources to protect all of you at all times from angry citizens. I suggest that you keep a low profile while we concern ourselves with winning this war."

"Finally, a few words about Martial Law. We have put that in place only in areas that are under attack, and we will not leave it in place for long. I know there are many out there who are concerned about the guarantees of Liberty which reside in our Constitution and Bill of Rights. This Administration takes those guarantees very seriously. Martial Law will only be declared when we need it to fight the enemy. Rumors of an extension of Martial Law to all areas of the United States are false. We have no reason to do that. We will not do that. I hope that puts these fears to rest. That is all for now, and sorry, but I won't take any questions at this time."

He left the podium and walked off to the right.

"That was a good response," Jefferson said.

"Yeah, if he really goes through with it," Brendan said. "And remember, he ain't *our* President anymore."

There were murmurs of agreement around the room.

Richardson was sitting there, eyes still on the TV, trying to ignore the chatter. Jefferson saw him. "Something bothering you, Richardson?"

"That was brilliant," he said. "Got to give the President credit."

"About what?" Jefferson asked.

"The knuckle-dragging Islamist said that his forces would use the laws of the democracies against us," Richardson said. "The President just headed that off at the pass with the words about moderate Muslims."

"How so?" Brendan asked.

Jefferson thought for a moment. "I get it," he said. "He's basically saying that moderate Muslims had better stay out of the way. He's cleared the field and activated private citizens to help. The radicals won't be able to hide behind the good people anymore."

The commentator came back on the TV screen.

"Oh, crap, that's London," Richardson said. A hush came over the room as the men watched video cameras pan over fires and people running around, pulling people to the ground.

"That amazing footage was taken in Westminster. About an hour ago, the British Secret Service foiled a nuclear attack on the city. It was another pleasure craft, on the Thames River. The device was disarmed and all suspects were apprehended. According to BBC they were of Pakistani and Syrian nationality."

"So what's that going on?" Brendan asked.

The announcer continued.

"As you can see, we have fires burning in the background. At the time that the news about the foiled nuclear attack was released, Islamic demonstrators were still camped outside Westminster Abbey. Men flooded out of the nearby pubs, beat most of the demonstrators to death, and burned their tents, signs, and other items. London police looked on, but took no action."

Jefferson and Richardson looked at each other and grinned. "The Brits have the same idea," Jefferson said. "Good."

The screen now went to another special bulletin. The tired commentators were back on, looking at papers on their desk.

"Ladies and Gentlemen, we have two more major stories to report. First, the United States Government has announced that it is moving into Mexico to take control of that country, in lieu of an official Mexican government. The agents from Venezuela who had

attempted to take over have fled that country after Mexican nationals stormed the Presidential Palace. The United States is coming in at the request of what is left of the Mexican government. They will not answer questions about the length of our occupation or plans for the future."

"You know what that means," Jefferson said.

"No, what?" Juan Carlos asked.

"The remaining troops from Venezuela will flee to the north," he said. "Right into our laps."

"Why would they do that?" Juan Carlos asked. "That's out of the frying pan and into the fire."

"Wait and see," Jefferson said. "A lot of them are gonna try to come through the gulf coast, and through here, since they won't be able to take over Mexico."

"The second story comes out of North and South Korea. United States and South Korean troops are evacuating from the border next to the de-militarized zone, at the same time that the Chinese are pulling their troops away from the northern border of North Korea. It is widely expected that a major attack is imminent, and sources say that North Korea is getting ready to fire their ICBMs in desperation. South Korea and Japan are trying to protect their people as best they can, and missile defense units are at the ready. Although untested, North Korean ICBMs do have the

capability to hit the western United States as well as the Russian Federation and other Asian countries."

"If those idiots manage to hit us with anything, it'll be pure luck," Brendan said.

"Don't be so sure," Jefferson said. "I've seen some of the recent intelligence. They're finally getting themselves up to early 1960s US technology. We had reliable ICBMs by then."

A few people chuckled.

"Yeah, but our missile defense is a lot better than it used to be," Richardson said.

"Hope you're right," Jefferson said. His phone rang. He paused and took it out of his pocket, looking at the number. "Be right back."

"Wonder who that is?" Juan Carlos asked as Jefferson left the room.

"Hopefully Gallagher telling him to let us go," Brendan said.

Jefferson ran back into the room and grabbed the remote to the TV. He turned it off.

"We've got incoming," he said. "That was Gallagher. The remainder of the Venezuelans are going for broke. They have enough aircraft to do some real damage. They're coming across in the northern half of the lake. Get in your boats and head for Government Cove, down by the dam. Don't stop and fight. Preserve yourselves and the boats. If aircraft are coming at you, get to the coastline and get away. That's an order."

"Where's our air support?" Richardson asked.

"The assets we have are busy in the north part of the lake, and now they're having to fight off Venezuelan Mig 29s. We have US Airforce assets on the way, but they won't be here in time to protect this base. Get the hell out of here now!"

The men got to their feet and headed for the door. They went into the cool dusk and broke into a run, making the docks in less than a minute.

Juan Carlos jumped into their boat and started the engine as Richardson and Brendan got the dock lines off. The other crews were getting into their boats all around them.

"Look, Captain Jefferson is getting into Boat 31," Brendan said as he jumped into the boat.

Juan Carlos nodded and backed the boat out of the slip. "Load the guns."

"On it," Brendan said. Richardson nodded and joined him.

Juan Carlos gunned the engine and headed out into the Lake at full bore, the other boats following. They could hear gunfire and explosions to the north.

"That doesn't sound very far away," Richardson shouted.

"Seriously," Juan Carlos said. "Let's keep our lights off."

"Yeah, definitely," Richardson said. Juan Carlos kept the boat as close to shore as he could and still go full blast. Richardson and Brendan had their eyes peeled into the sky. Suddenly there was a flash and explosion behind them.

"Dammit, they just hit the headquarters building," Richardson said, looking back.

"Keep up the speed," Brendon said. "Don't stop for anything."

"Get out the SMAW," Juan Carlos said. "I can't be on the M-19 and drive at the same time when the enemy is behind us."

"Good idea," Richardson said. "We could take out a chopper with one of those rockets."

Brendan took the SMAW and several rockets out of the storage locker and loaded it. Richardson kept his eyes in the darkening sky as the boat flew over the glassy water, flanked on both sides by the other boats.

"Don't feel right to be running, dude," Juan Carlos said.

"We'll fight another day," Richardson said.

To be continued in Bug Out! Texas Book 3!

ABOUT THE AUTHOR

Robert G Boren is a writer from the South Bay section of Southern California. He writes Short Stories, Novels, and Serialized Fiction.

Made in the USA
Las Vegas, NV
23 January 2021

"Govern wisely, and as little as possible".

—Sam Houston